The INVISIBLE DETECTIVE

DOUBLE LIFE

by Justin Richards

G. P. PUTNAM'S SONS · NEW YORK

ACKNOWLEDGMENTS

*I am indebted to my family—Alison, Julian and Christian—
for their patience, comments and love, and to my U.K. editor,
Stephen Cole, for his comments, patience and confidence.*

G. P. PUTNAM'S SONS

A division of Penguin Young Readers Group. Published by The Penguin Group.
Penguin Group (USA) Inc., 375 Hudson Street, New York, NY 10014, U.S.A.
Penguin Group (Canada), 10 Alcorn Avenue, Toronto, Ontario, Canada M4V 3B2
(a division of Pearson Penguin Canada Inc.). Penguin Books Ltd, 80 Strand, London
WC2R 0RL, England. Penguin Ireland, 25 St. Stephen's Green, Dublin 2, Ireland
(a division of Penguin Books Ltd.). Penguin Group (Australia), 250 Camberwell Road,
Camberwell, Victoria 3124, Australia (a division of Pearson Australia Group Pty Ltd).
Penguin Books India Pvt Ltd, 11 Community Centre, Panchsheel Park,
New Delhi - 110 017, India. Penguin Group (NZ), Cnr Airborne and Rosedale Roads,
Albany, Auckland 1310, New Zealand (a division of Pearson New Zealand Ltd).
Penguin Books (South Africa) (Pty) Ltd, 24 Sturdee Avenue, Rosebank, Johannesburg 2196,
South Africa. Penguin Books Ltd, Registered Offices: 80 Strand, London WC2R 0RL, England.

Design by Marikka Tamura. Text set in Folio Medium and Baskerville Book.

Library of Congress Cataloging-in-Publication Data
Richards, Justin. Double life / Justin Richards. p. cm. – (The Invisible Detective)
Summary: After finding a mysterious stone and an old casebook, fourteen-year-old Arthur finds himself
remembering the 1936 adventures of a boy named Art who, under the identity of the Invisible Detective,
works with three friends in London to solve the mystery of sinister puppets who are replacing real people.
[1. Zombies–Fiction. 2. Puppets–Fiction. 3. Extrasensory perception–Fiction. 4. Grandfathers–Fiction.
5. London (England)–History–20th century–Fiction. 6. Horror stories. 7. Mystery and detective stories.]
I. Title. PZ7.R386Do 2005 [Fic]–dc22 2004009536 ISBN 0-399-24313-5
1 3 5 7 9 10 8 6 4 2
First Impression

For Terrance Dicks,
who taught a generation of children
about adventures
and the reward of reading.

PROLOGUE

The other kids thought the place was haunted, but Arthur Drake never believed stuff like that. He walked past the antiques shop on Cannon Street every day on his way to and from school, and whether it was haunted or not, he never had the slightest desire to go inside.

Anyway, it was always closed. Which was probably how it had got the reputation. The faded shop front was strangely out of place among the glass and steel of the offices and banks that now surrounded and overshadowed it.

If you peered through the grubby, misted windows into the dusty interior, you could just make out the piles of bric-a-brac heaped around the cluttered room. Whatever ghosts you might see would be reflections of people passing on the other side of the street, or, if you were lucky, a furtive glimpse of the elusive shopkeeper.

Arthur had seen him once. He was unlocking the door one morning as Arthur bolted past, late for the bell. A short man with wispy gray hair that had thinned almost to nothing. His eyes were enlarged by round, wire-rimmed pebble glasses as he fixed Arthur with a surprised stare, as if the sight of a fourteen-year-old boy who was late for school was a rare sight.

It was only when Arthur met him again that he began to realize why the old man had stared at him.

It was pouring. "Raining bats and frogs," as his dad would

say. The morning had been bright and clear, so Arthur hadn't bothered with a raincoat. He held his plastic folder of homework over his head as he ran, blinking away the rain that angled in at his face.

He was so surprised that he just stopped and stared. The rain continued to pummel down, and he could feel it soaking through his jacket now. But his attention was focused on the antiques shop.

He had never seen its door open before. Without even knowing what he was doing, he stepped inside.

He was never exactly sure why he did it. Perhaps it was to get out of the rain, or maybe he was just curious. Maybe it was so he'd have something to tell the others the next day—something to give him a bit of cred in the playground, a story to tell over lunch. Or maybe it was fate. Except that Arthur didn't believe in stuff like that.

Not yet.

Inside, the shop looked exactly as you would have expected from the street. There was as much dust in the air as there was grime on the windows, so it still seemed misty and vague. He picked his way between piles of ancient books in heavy leather covers and squeezed past a dark wooden table that was struggling to support a mountain of boxes and jars. A huge gray moth stared at him from inside a glass-fronted display case on the wall. Or was it a butterfly that was so dusty all its color had leached away? The edges of the room were lost in shadows, as if the shop went on forever.

There was a table with a chessboard of light and dark

wooden squares laid into it. The pieces were set out in midgame. Ivory or bone. Wasn't ivory banned now? A drop of water fell onto the board as Arthur leaned over to look more closely. He wiped it away guiltily, leaving a smear of rich texture across the middle of the dull wood and a layer of black on the edge of his hand.

Arthur looked up, worried that someone might have seen him. Although it was a shop, he felt somehow that he was intruding. The shopkeeper was standing just the other side of the board, for all the world like Arthur's opponent in the chess game, waiting to make his move.

"I—I'm sorry," Arthur stammered, looking down at the smeary mess on the board. "It's raining." He swallowed.

"So I see." The old man's voice was cracked and hoarse, as dusty as everything else in the place.

"I'd better be going."

The man shook his head, the edges of a smile creeping onto his face. "There's no hurry. Please, take your time. Look around. Wait for the rain to ease off."

"OK. Right. Thanks." Somehow Arthur was less interested now. A minute ago, looking around had seemed mysterious and thrilling, but now it was just a shop. Until the man spoke again, and then his quiet words sent a shiver of cold through Arthur's body.

"You are always welcome in this shop, Arthur Drake," the old man said.

CHAPTER I

On a summer's evening long before that rainy day, when the shop was still a locksmith's and Arthur's father had not yet been born, a new king sat alone in his palace in London and contemplated the future. His own circumstances were changing as quickly as the world outside. Across Europe, a general called Franco was fighting a civil war in Spain. In Germany, a former corporal called Adolf Hitler was planning a war that would set the world ablaze. In the United States a little girl with a squeaky voice captured the hearts of moviegoers, and in a street in the West End of London a dashing adventurer called Simon Templar helped a fallen woman to her feet.

But none of this mattered to King Edward VIII. His empire was waning and his own thoughts had turned from politics and grief to love and sadness. It mattered no more to him that Shirley Temple had been awarded an Oscar than it did that the first Spitfire had completed its air trials. But he knew that soon—very soon now—he would have to face up to the fact that he could not keep both his love and his throne.

On the desk in front of him, *The Times* was folded open at a short leader article that discussed allegations about his friendship with a woman called Mrs. Simpson. His fingers drummed a slow beat on the newsprint, gradually picking up the ink and smudging the headline. Further down the page, a seven-line snippet covered rumors of an "invisible detective" called Brandon Lake operating in London. But the king had not read it.

Even if he had read the short article, he would not have cared that in a small room above a locksmith's shop off Cannon Street the curtains were drawn. A group of people stood, sat and perched in silence and awe as they waited for the Invisible Detective to speak.

A single electric table lamp cast a dusty glow across the grubby wallpaper. It threw the silent figures into elongated shadows and deepened the gloom in the corners of the room. A stray strand of yellowed evening light crept in through a small gap between the mildewed curtains, illuminating impatient feet.

Behind the same curtains, Jonny Levin held his breath and a fishing rod. He shrugged into the bay of the window to escape being seen. He strained to hear what the detective said, leaning as far as he dared in the direction of the old armchair that faced the window and kept its back coyly toward the assembly.

The chair was a faded burgundy, though you could not tell that in the gloom. Its seat had almost worn through and the threadbare wings that swept forward from the high back and helped to conceal its occupant were raddled with dust. All that could be seen of the person in the chair was the shadow of a hand. A hand that gestured and punctuated the detective's speech. A shadow that gave away nothing about the detective himself.

Jonny knew who was in the chair, but the atmosphere still infected him. He was dying to scratch his nose, but dared not move his hand. He was itching to take a deep breath, but knew that the dust from the curtain would make him cough. Above all, he was desperate to remain hidden. So desperate that he failed to notice the twitch of the material in front of him as another slight figure stepped silently behind the curtain; failed to hear the faint scuff of feet on the bare boards beside him; failed to see the pale hand that snaked its way toward his shoulder until it touched him.

Then he gasped, struggled not to cough and bit his tongue to keep himself from crying out all in the same moment as he almost dropped his fishing rod. But Meg's hand held his shoulder firm and kept him upright. She shook her head in annoyance.

"Ah, yes." The deep voice of Brandon Lake was muffled slightly by the curtains, but his words were clear. "At our last consulting session, I recall that Mrs. Simms enquired about her nephew, Andrew Baxter. It seems that he had been missing from home the previous night. This was unusual, but Mr. and Mrs. Baxter were reluctant to call the police. Mrs. Simms, you will recall, persuaded them that my more discreet services might be useful."

The room was silent. Everyone there knew what had happened. News traveled fast in this part of London.

"Is Mrs. Simms with us today?" Brandon Lake continued.

"Over here, sir."

Jonny strained to hear. The woman's voice was quiet and nervous.

"Thank you, sir. You saved the poor lad's life, you did, and no mistake."

The reaction of the assembly was difficult to judge from where Jonny was hiding. There was some quiet muttering, but there was also a "shushing" and a shuffling of interested feet.

Brandon Lake waited for calm before he replied. "An interesting case," he said slowly. "May I ask how the poor child is after his ordeal?"

"Oh, he's fine, sir. Leg's mending, the doctor says."

There was a hint of satisfaction in the detective's voice now. "I am only glad that I was able to help."

"That's a bit rich," Jonny murmured. He knew who had done the real work.

Beside him, Meg dug her elbow into his ribs. "You know he means all of us, the whole gang," she whispered back. "Not just Arthur Drake. You and me too. And Flinch."

Jonny did not reply. She was right of course. And anyway, the detective was speaking again.

"Yes, a most satisfactory outcome for all concerned. Let us hope that Andrew makes a full recovery very shortly."

Jonny could remember last Tuesday's excitement. Meg was right, they had all played a part.

The previous Tuesday had been cool and dry. The light breeze had whipped away some of London's stink and the sun burned off the early mist by midday. Art had spent the morning talking to the kids Andrew had played with on the Sunday evening, trying to discover who had seen him last and where. Georgie Thomas had left the boy behind the steelworks at All Hallows. They'd arranged to meet the next day, though Andrew never showed up.

But by then his parents were worried and the Invisible Detective was on the case. It was up to Jonny and Meg to retrace the route Andrew Baxter should have taken home. They looked a mismatched pair as they walked together along the narrow streets behind the steelworks. Jonny was slight, with thin dark hair slicked close over his head. His prominent nose and angular features seemed more pronounced given his relatively small size. He was not much younger than Meg, though she looked much older, being bigger.

Meg's bulky clothes hid the shape of her thirteen-year-old body, and she always wore long sleeves and high-necked collars. She liked to cover as much of herself as she could. Her auburn hair was a riotous cascade that curled over her shoulders, the warm color at odds with her usually sour expression. Jonny knew that when the sun shone through her hair, it seemed to glow—just as he knew that on the rare occasions when she did smile, her face lit up like a saint's.

They had already walked from Andrew's house to where he was last seen, asking if anyone remembered him—a nine-year-old boy, running home late for tea on Sunday evening. But nobody who was willing to answer could help them. So they turned around and started back toward Andrew's house with lumps of disappointment in their stomachs.

There was a small yard just off the passage. High walls on either side, no doorways. Jonny could hear a rhythmic thumping from the direction of the river and he thought at first it was the steelworks or maybe the railway. But as they looked into the yard they found a boy kicking a scuffed leather football against the wall. He was perhaps ten years old, ragged and in need of a wash. He waited for the ball to bounce on the ground in front of him, then punted it back at the wall.

Jonny made to move on, but Meg held his arm. She nodded toward the urchin. "Maybe he saw the kid?"

Jonny shrugged. "We can ask."

"Ask what?" The ball bounced away into a corner as the boy turned toward them. "It's my ball," he assured them with an anxious expression.

"No, it isn't," Meg said at once.

"How d'you know?"

"She just knows," Jonny said. "But that's not what we wanted."

"What, then?"

"Have you seen a boy?" Meg asked him. "Sunday evening. About six o'clock?"

"Might have. What's he look like?"

"He's called Andrew," Jonny said. "He was playing near here, but he never got home."

The scruffy boy laughed at that. "I never go home neither," he said. "What's the point?"

"He's nine. With fair hair, lots of freckles. Wearing gray shorts and a white shirt."

The boy went to retrieve his football. "Didn't know he was called Andrew."

"So you have seen him," Meg said.

"Now and again. Not sure about Sunday though. He stops to kick about sometimes." The ball struck the brickwork, bounced. "He likes to climb up the wall too. He runs along the top and jumps down into the next yard. Says it's a shortcut."

It took Jonny several minutes to haul himself to the top of the wall. The bricks were old and crumbling, so there were plenty of footholds, but the wall was almost twelve feet high. He hardly dared look down. Certainly he didn't intend to stand on the top, let alone run along. Instead, he sat astride the wall. The surface was uneven and large sections had broken away, leaving ragged edges like huge bite marks.

He could see down into the next courtyard and through to the street beyond. He could see the river on the other side of the wall. The ground sloped away, so the drop was nearer twenty feet that side. There was a stretch of wasteland down to the water's edge. Nowhere for a nine-year-old boy to be lying hurt. Except for the culvert. It was angled so that the large opening was in shadow. It seemed to be an overflow, allowing water from the sewers or drains to run off into the river. If Andrew Baxter had slipped on the wall and fallen, he might have landed inside the dark opening, out of sight and goodness only knew how far down.

"Hello," Jonny shouted. He cupped his hands around his mouth to try to funnel his voice toward the culvert. "Andrew, are you there? Are you hurt?"

"Can you see him?" Meg called up excitedly from below.

"No. But I can see where he might be. If he fell."

"Can you get down the other side?"

Jonny considered. "No, I don't think so. It's too smooth that side and it's a lot further down. The yard's been banked up or something. Maybe it floods."

"So what now?" Meg wondered, as Jonny climbed back down into the yard.

The boy let the ball roll away from him. "There's a hole in the wall, you know," he said. "Over here. Lost a ball through it once." He grinned, and Jonny could see that one of his front teeth was a blackened mess. "That was my ball and all."

The hole was at the bottom of the wall in the corner of the yard. It looked as if it was there to allow water to drain away, and Jonny could tell that the yard sloped slightly down toward that corner. He could see the drop to the ground on the other side—perhaps six or eight feet. He could also see into the culvert from here. And he could see what might—just *might*—be the shadowy silhouette of a small figure. He moved aside so that Meg could take a look.

"That's him," she said at once.

"It might be," Jonny said dubiously. It was just a shape. "It could be anything."

"It's him," Meg insisted. She was a year older than Jonny, but she wanted to seem older still. She was in charge of their little gang, the Cannoniers. After Art, of course. "I know it is."

Jonny hoped she was right, for the boy's sake. But he also wanted to tell her that he didn't care if she knew or not, if she was certain or just guessing. He wanted to tell her he knew about the bruises on her arm that she'd pulled her sleeves down to hide, that he would listen all day if she wanted to tell him why she never smiled, why she hated to go home.

But his thoughts were interrupted by the scruffy boy elbowing him aside so he could look as well. "You'll never get through there, though," the boy told them. "You're too big. So am I. Never got my ball back."

But Jonny was looking at Meg, and he could tell she

was thinking the same as him. "Flinch," he said. And she nodded.

Buildings, pedestrians, street hawkers: all were a blur to Jonny as he passed them. His head was down, his arms pumping, his chest heaving. He could hear the shouts as he almost collided with other people on the pavement, but he hadn't the breath to apologize. He had to be quick. And he had to find Flinch.

He passed the station and was heading toward Southwark Bridge when he felt the flicking at his feet. He glanced down, swerving to avoid a woman in a bright green hat. His shoelace was slapping across the pavement with every step. It whipped up around his ankle as he raced along. He tried to ignore it, but in the back of his mind he could hear his father chiding him, telling him how dangerous it was. "Could have a nasty fall. Only takes a moment to do it up."

So he skidded to a halt at the end of Dowgate Hill and bent to retie it. As he straightened up and set off again he thought of Flinch, alone on the streets or wrapped in a thin blanket in the warehouse on Cannon Street where the gang met. Thought of how nobody ever told *her* to do up her shoelaces. Thought of her tear-smudged face and her stained clothing and how eager she always was to help. And before he knew it he was standing in front of the Cannoniers' den, rasping for breath and hoping Flinch was waiting nearby.

It took him a moment to spot her. She was leaning against a wall on the shady side of the street. Flinch was a pale girl, small and thin. Her clothes were torn and grimy and her straggly blond hair was stained almost brown. She stood so still that she seemed almost to blend into the cracked brickwork. She smiled as Jonny approached, her young face lighting up suddenly as her eyes widened.

He took a few moments to catch his breath, gasping out his news. Flinch nodded, serious now as she listened.

"I'll get my breath back and catch you up," Jonny told her. "If he's there, we can tell the police and they can take a boat in. Go as fast as you can."

"I'll be quick, Jonny," she told him. "Honest, I will." Her whole body was shaking with anticipation and excitement.

The gap between the bricks was only about a foot wide. Flinch pushed and squeezed her body through the narrow opening. She could feel her left shoulder catching on the edge and wriggled until she heard a click. The loose limpness in her arm told her that the joint had dislocated. She edged forward and this time her shoulders fitted between the bricks.

"That's neat," a voice called from the yard behind her. "Here, see if you can find my ball, will you?"

Arms out in front of her, Flinch clicked her shoulder back in and let herself fall forward. She kept the backs of her knees hooked around the brickwork, reaching down toward the ground below. It was still a long drop—maybe three feet.

"You all right, Flinch?" Meg called from behind her.

"Yeah," she called back, and let herself drop. She broke the fall with her hands, rolling as she landed. The ground was damp and the long grass softened her impact.

Flinch leaped to her feet and ran quickly to the edge of the culvert. Carefully, she leaned forward and peered into the shadows. She could see the light reflecting off the water as it rippled far below.

"Who are you?" a weak voice asked. "Are you the monster?"

"Course not," Flinch said. She could dimly see the shape of the boy lying in the shallow water below her. "Are you Andrew?"

"I seen it last night," the boy went on. "Lay very still, closed my eyes tight till it went. I think maybe I fell asleep. Perhaps I dreamed it." He paused, before adding, "Yes, I'm Andrew. Andrew Baxter."

"Are you all right?" Flinch couldn't see a way down, not safely. "I'll have to get some help."

The dark shape struggled to lift itself into a sitting position. "I think my leg's busted. I fell. Couldn't get out again. There's a dead cat down here too," he said. "Stinks to high heaven. Who are you?"

Flinch was already turning away. "The Invisible Detective sent me," she said.

She just caught the boy's weak, faint words as she ran

back toward the hole in the wall. "Wow! The Invisible Detective!"

"How do you know my name?" Arthur stood frozen in the musty shop, caught in midturn.

"I have always known it." The old man seemed surprised at the question. He picked up one of the chess pieces, a white knight, and peered closely at it. After a moment's examination, he blew off a mist of dust, nodded with satisfaction and replaced it on the clean round patch it had left on its square.

"What?"

But the old man clearly thought that his answer was sufficient. "Did you know," he said as he blew the dust off the other white knight, "that the Invisible Detective used to hold his consulting sessions here?"

It seemed such a strange thing to say that Arthur was stumped for a reply. He shook his head.

"Well, not here in this room, but upstairs. Oh, yes." The shopkeeper stared into the distance, the murky light reflecting off his thick glasses. "It was a locksmith's shop back then, back in the 1930s." He nodded to himself, then turned to stare at Arthur through those pebble lenses. "But of course you know all about that. All about the Invisible Detective."

"No," Arthur managed to say, though his voice was a squeaky croak. "No, I've never heard of him."

The old man was not listening. He was picking his way across the room toward a back corner. He paused long enough to beckon for Arthur to follow, then resumed his journey. "Over here, over here. Come on, come on," he called as the boy hesitated.

"Why not?" Arthur muttered. He could see the rain leaving tracks down the windows. If anything, it had got worse since he came in. He followed the man across the shop, trying to find a path through the dusty piles and the pieces of ancient furniture.

"I've got something here that will interest you."

CHAPTER 2

Jonny drifted back to the present as the Invisible Detective took questions and problems for the following week. The first few were the usual fare—a missing cat not seen for three days, the question of how Michael Groat's new front door got plastered in mud, Mrs. Haskins's concern about what her husband was really doing when he told her he was working late at the insurance office . . .

Then came a question from Harry Walker. The man had a nasal, high-pitched voice that made Jonny's head ring as he introduced himself. "I'd like to know," he whined, "if it isn't too much trouble, I'd like to know why the clock of Christ Church, Spitalfields, chimed only five times at six o'clock yesterday morning. The locals are saying it's a sign from God. Is that right?"

Beside Jonny, Meg stiffened as the man spoke.

"That is indeed an intriguing question," the detective said.

But Jonny's attention was all on Meg. Her face had creased into a frown of concentration as she elbowed him aside and stepped up to the crack in the curtains. Her head jogged back and forth as she struggled to get a glimpse of Harry Walker.

"Yeah, well," came the self-satisfied whine, "what do your deductive powers say about that, then?"

"He's lying," Meg hissed to Jonny. She pointed at his

fishing rod. "Trying it on. Clocks striking the wrong number, my foot."

For a second, Jonny was afraid that she would stamp her foot to make the point. He lifted his free hand to try to calm her, but Meg was already producing a slip of paper from her sleeve and scribbling on the back of it with a chewed pencil stub. As soon as she was done, she thrust the paper at Jonny and gesticulated violently for him to act. Quickly, he attached the paper to the fishhook.

Jonny gave the fishing rod a quick, well-practiced flick. The line paid out silently as the hook spun across the room toward the nearby armchair. A moment later there was a shrill cry of surprise and pain from the same direction. This was followed immediately by the sound of shuffling feet and murmurings from the people in the room. Jonny looked around and found Meg still glaring at him. "Sorry," he mouthed.

"I'll pay my sixpence, sir," Walker protested from beyond the curtain.

"That's all right," the detective replied, his composure and baritone regained. "The process, the means by which I can sit here and ponder and deduce the answers to your questions, is a difficult one. It calls for precise and constant meditation, and it is not without hazard. Or occasionally pain."

There were gasps from the assembled observers. Jonny smiled weakly and Meg rolled her eyes. The fishing line jerked twice in rapid succession and Jonny reeled it back in.

To his surprise, the paper was still attached to the hook. He exchanged a nervous glance with Meg, then removed it. From the other side of the curtain, Jonny could hear murmuring and excited whispers of anticipation.

Before he could examine the folded paper, Meg had snatched it from him. She opened it, quickly read what was inside, then folded it up again and handed it back to Jonny.

He opened the paper carefully. There were several lines of spidery pencil writing. It was Meg's writing—the note she had sent. But across the middle of it, in heavier, thicker pencil, was scrawled a single word in large block capitals: OUCH.

For a moment, Jonny considered writing "Sorry" on the paper and sending it back, but the detective was already speaking again.

"An intriguing mystery indeed," he said slowly. "A clock that does not know its own time. And in Spitalfields of all places."

Now that he knew, Jonny could hear that the sounds he had taken for anticipation and excitement might as easily be amusement and mockery. They'd laugh on the other sides of their faces soon, though.

"It is as I thought." There was a hush, and Jonny knew it was of awed anticipation. Then the detective went on, his tone now severe and dark. "Don't try to play the fool with me, Mr. Walker. You are a fraud and a liar, and I do not take kindly to being tested in this manner."

Jonny strained to listen, but all he heard was silence from the people on the other side of the curtains.

"I would deem it a favor," the detective said brusquely, "if you would leave us now, Mr. Walker. Perhaps someone else has a more serious question?"

Another voice spoke up, talking over the sound of Harry Walker's shuffling footsteps as he made his way to the door and down the stairs. "I have a serious question, sir. Albert Norris, the name is."

"Ah, Mr. Albert Norris," the detective said with evident satisfaction. "You are, I believe, the proprietor of the Dog and Goose pub here on Cannon Street."

Compared with some of Brandon Lake's deductions, this one was rather tame, but it still drew a gasp of astonished appreciation.

" 'S'right, sir," the gruff voice proclaimed. "Best pint of ale in town."

The detective laughed politely. "I doubt that these people need me to tell them that," he said. This drew further laughter and cries of appreciation. "What is your question for the next session, Mr. Norris?"

"Well, it's about Reggie Yarmouth, sir. He's a local. That is, I dunno if he lives around here, but he drinks at the Dog every night on his way home from work. Every night, six days a week, without fail."

"You are enquiring about the state of his liver perhaps? Or his wallet?"

Another ripple of laughter. But Albert Norris's voice was serious as he answered. "Well, he does owe a tab, sir, I won't deny that. But he hasn't been in all week. I just thought, what with finding young Baxter and all . . ." Norris was a big man, almost as broad as he was around. His equally huge moustache twitched with embarrassment as he went on, "I ain't worried about the money, not really. But, well, Reggie's a nice enough geezer. Not big on conversation, but he likes his pint and he props up the bar. And he's there every night."

"But not this week? A holiday perhaps."

Norris was dubious. "Don't seem likely, sir. I mean, it's possible, but he would have said. I'm sure he would. He left last Tuesday and said he'd see us Wednesday. But he's never been back in."

"An illness, then," the detective decided. "Mr. Yarmouth is indisposed."

"I thought of that, sir. And I'm sure you're right. Only . . ." His voice tailed off.

"You are worried about him."

"Yes, sir," Norris admitted, his voice barely more than a mumble. "Not a big talker, like I said. And he's got a funny way of wiping his mouth—with his little finger all curled up like—when he finishes his pint. Fair drives me mad, it does. But he's been coming into the Dog for ten years or more."

"Then perhaps there is indeed cause for concern," the

detective said slowly. "Now it is time to adjourn for this week. And in addition to the other problems with which you have presented me today, if Mr. Yarmouth is still missing by this time next week, then I shall have further information as to his condition."

People were already edging out of the door and starting down the stairs. Norris's relieved voice boomed above the sound of their footsteps. "Thank you, sir. You're a gent, sir, and no mistake." Then he too turned and followed the crowd back down to Cannon Street.

The voices of the departing people carried up the stairs to Meg and Jonny as they stepped out from behind the curtains and drew them back.

"Always gets me, how he knows that stuff."

"How's he do it, then? Tell me that."

"Remember how he knew when Josh Farmer had run away to join the army?"

"What about how Stan Compton bought that strychnine the week before his wife had the cramps?"

The stories faded. Some of them were true, some rumor and gossip. They all added to the reputation and the mystery of the Invisible Detective. "Invisible" because nobody ever saw Brandon Lake in the dim light of the room. Nobody ever saw him arrive, and despite several people having stayed outside to watch, nobody ever saw him leave.

There was a simple reason for this.

Brandon Lake, the Invisible Detective, did not exist.

If any of the people who had crowded into the room above the locksmith's had stayed behind unseen, if anyone other than Meg and Jonny had watched as the curtains were drawn back, they would have been surprised at what they saw.

The figure in the chair rose and staggered clumsily to his feet. His movements were hampered by the heavy coat that he was wearing—a coat that was far too big for the small figure inside. Arthur Drake shrugged out of the coat and heaved it over the back of the chair. He coughed to loosen his throat, which was sore from deepening his voice, and flicked his head to move his dark brown hair away from his high forehead.

"Good session, Art," Meg said.

"Very good," Jonny agreed.

Art nodded. He was tall for his fourteen years, but slightly built. He smiled at his friends. "All down to your investigations," he told them in his precise and measured voice. "I'm just the mouthpiece."

"Oh, come on, Art," Meg chided him. "You *are* the Invisible Detective. We all know that. Even Flinch."

"Especially Flinch," Jonny added. Meg sometimes forgot why they had invented Brandon Lake. "She got bored and went back to the den," he told Art.

"But you spotted that Harry Walker was a phony," Art said to Meg. "It's incredible how you do that."

Meg's face lit up, a rare smile that only Art could coax from her.

Art turned to Jonny. "So how much did we make this week?"

Jonny had already checked the tin on the chair by the door. He was the treasurer, better with sums than any of the others—even Art. "After the rent for the room," he said, "it's two shillings and sixpence. Half a crown, exactly."

"Not bad," Art said appreciatively. He winced as he spoke and his hand went to his cheek. He dabbed at it. "Yes, that was a good session. But if you ever hook me like a fish again, Jonny, I'll brain you."

"Sorry, Art."

Art laughed and slapped the younger boy on the shoulder. "Only kidding. Come on. I need to settle up with Mr. Jerrickson for the use of the room. And Flinch will be waiting." He paused at the top of the stairs, sad and thoughtful. Meg put her hand on his arm. "I hope we'll have enough to get her some new clothes before the winter sets in," he said.

Flinch was already on the stairs, her eyes wide and tears welling up.

At once Art was with her. "What is it, Flinch? What's the matter?"

"The den," she stammered through her suppressed sobs. "I been to the warehouse. I was going to wait for you there." She turned away so they wouldn't see her cry.

"There's someone at our den," she said. "With vans and boxes and all." Her voice cracked slightly. "And they're carrying in dead bodies."

Eventually Arthur found himself standing beside the little shopkeeper, looking down into a display case. The lid was so layered with dirt and dust that it was impossible to see inside. When the man opened it, he sent a gray cloud up into the air. The interior of the case was lined with faded red velvet and held just two things. The man lifted one of them out carefully and handed it to Arthur. It was a notebook. The binding was cracked leather and there was a hint of gold lettering on the front, though it had long since faded beyond the point where it could be read. Arthur turned it over in his hands. He looked at the old man, who was nodding and smiling at him encouragingly.

So Arthur opened the book. The pages were unlined, made of thick cartridge paper. As he leafed through, he could see that each one was covered in writing, with occasional sketches and scribbles. The dark ink had faded, but it was legible enough. The writing was pretty untidy. Some sections seemed neater than others. Some were obviously a hurried scrawl.

His mind in a fog, Arthur turned to the inside front cover and the first page. Sure enough, there was a title:

The Casebook of the Invisible Detective
as kept by
Arthur Drake and the Cannoniers
(1936–   )

Arthur stared in disbelief. "But that's my name," he heard himself saying.

"Of course." The shopkeeper sounded pleased with himself.

A space had been left for the end date, but never filled in. Underneath, in smaller writing, was an address that Arthur recognized.

He stared at it, shaking his head. This just made no sense. No sense at all. "It's impossible," he said quietly. "Impossible."

"Oh?"

"It's my name," he repeated, leafing through the brittle pages once more. "And my address."

The old man was nodding again, his glasses glinting as the light caught the movement. "Anything else you notice?" he asked, his creaking voice full of anticipation.

"Yes," Arthur admitted, though he hardly dared to say it. "This is my handwriting."

CHAPTER 3

There was a row of houses opposite the warehouse. They were small, terraced houses, bunched together with doorways no more than a few paces apart. Art and the others stood in the shadows of one of these doorways, out of sight from the other side of the street.

While they waited, Art finished writing up his notes from the session. He had a leather-bound notebook in which he proudly kept track of all the Invisible Detective's work. His "casebook." Now he held Flinch's shoulders as she stood close in front of him. He could feel her trembling through the thin material of her grubby dress. Beside him, Meg's face was set in the stony expression she wore when she did not want to show what she was thinking or feeling—which was most of the time. Jonny kicked his feet nervously and sniffed as they watched.

A lorry was parked outside the warehouse, obscuring their view of most of the front, but they could see the main doors. It was the first time that Art had seen the huge wooden doors standing open. The Cannoniers used to let themselves in through a side door where the wood had rotted from around the lock. It was strange to be able to see right into the unloading area at the front of the building. Even more odd to watch as the men carried in packing cases, tea crates, all manner of materials.

And the bodies.

Flinch had been right. There were dozens of them, stiff and rigid and wrapped in sheets and blankets. The three men doing the unloading carried them through as if they were part and parcel of the furnishings. A stiff pale leg stuck out from beneath a blanket as another was carried inside. They couldn't really be dead bodies, Art decided—not to be carried around in full view, with jokes and laughter. Could they?

His thoughts were interrupted as the door behind him swung suddenly open and a brush cracked down on his head. He cried out and stepped quickly aside as the bristles tore at his cheeks. The brush swung after him like an angry cobra.

"What do you think you're doing, hanging around here?" The woman's face was wrinkled like an old apple. Her voice was hoarse and challenging. She stared at Art and the others as they jumped off her doorstep.

"Oh, it's you," she croaked accusingly. "Seen you lot hanging around before, I have." She nodded violently to prove it was true. "Up to no good. Stealing, I expect."

Art opened his mouth to protest. He had never stolen anything—at least, not without putting it back after proper examination. He knew the same was true of the others, apart from Flinch. But she only stole when she had to.

He did not get the chance to answer. The broom was striking again. Jonny was already off and Meg was dragging at Art's arm. Flinch backed away, terrified.

"Be off with you! Go on, get along!" The woman's

fierce dark eyes caught the light as she stepped forward. They glinted like a rat's.

Jonny was waiting three doors down. He grinned nervously as Flinch ran to join him. Meg and Art stamped after her. Art was seething.

"Stealing! Who does she think she is?" he demanded.

"We *were* on her step," Jonny pointed out.

"She could have asked us to move. Politely."

Meg laughed at the suggestion. But there was no humor in the sound.

"I should tell my d—" Art started to say. But he bit his tongue. "Nothing," he went on quickly. "Nothing. Forget I said that." He looked away from his friends, turning his attention back to the warehouse that had been their den.

"I suppose we'll have to find somewhere else," Jonny said.

"We'll still be the Cannoniers, though, won't we?" Flinch asked, her voice small and worried. "Even if it's not on Cannon Street?"

"We're not moving," Art said solemnly.

"We can't stay," Meg pointed out.

"We don't know yet, do we?" Art replied. "I want to know what's going on in there first."

"And how do we do that?" Jonny demanded. "Ask the Invisible Detective?"

Art was about to respond when a cab pulled quickly around the corner and drove past them. It drew up behind the lorry. Immediately, the back door opened and a tall, thin man leaped out. He reached back in to help another, smaller figure out of the vehicle.

"Perhaps now we'll find out what's going on," Art said quietly as they watched.

The second figure was a girl. She wore a long, dark red coat that reached almost to the ground. Despite the warmth of the evening, a hood trimmed with white fur was pulled up over her head and Art caught a glimpse of her delicate, shy face as she turned to thank the man. Her eyes were large and, for the briefest moment, Art thought she had stared right at him. But she continued to turn.

The man was already striding purposefully toward the open doors of the warehouse. The girl lurched after him, her walk an ungainly shuffle that seemed to take an effort and an age.

Meg was tugging at Art's sleeve. "I said, how do we find out?" she repeated.

Art smiled at his friends. "It's our warehouse," he said simply. "So we go in and see what they're up to."

The broken windows across the front had been boarded up. Undeterred, Art led the others down the side alley to the door they usually used. He was disappointed, though not surprised, to find that this too had been boarded shut. A plank of wood was nailed across it.

"We could pull it off," Meg suggested.

"They'd hear us," Jonny said. He was always the nervous one. His whole body was tense, as if he expected to be caught at any moment. "They'd notice. They'd know."

Meg glared at him.

"Come on," Art said, and kept walking. He took them around to the back of the building. The smell of the river was stronger here. And the drains. He ignored it and scanned the rear wall of the warehouse.

"There." He pointed. "Remember when we first came here, before the wood rotted away around the lock on that door?"

"I used to climb in through that window," Flinch recalled with pleasure. "And let you in through the door."

The back door to the warehouse had heavy bolts at the top and bottom. But it was easy to open from the inside.

"Oh, come on," Jonny protested. "That was over a year ago. Flinch was tiny then. She had to stand on a box to reach the top bolt." He turned to Flinch. "Didn't you?" he demanded.

She turned away. "I can do it," she said quietly. "I can still do it."

"Let's at least give it a try," Meg said. "If Flinch says she can do it . . ."

"Yes," Art said, "Flinch can give it a go. And if she gets through easily, then that's great. We have a look and see what's going on." He gently turned Flinch back to face him. "But . . . if you're not sure, or there are people inside, then come straight down again and I'll think of something else. All right?"

Flinch grinned. "Right." Her feet were beating a rhythm as she itched to get started. "Give us a leg up, Art!"

The window was even smaller than it had looked from six feet below. Flinch could remember that she used to fit through easily. It was tighter now—she had grown, and regular food from the others had made her generally larger all around. But she was certain she could do it.

The latch was loose and she could recall exactly how to jiggle the window to work it free. Since it had a latch, this window had not been boarded up by the warehouse's new tenants.

Inside was dusty and dark. It was a small storeroom or office. Flinch slipped through and dropped lightly to the wooden floor. She hesitated long enough to listen for any sounds of life and click her shoulder back into place before skipping happily to the door. She opened it carefully and ran down the short flight of bare wooden steps that led to ground level. She was delighted to find that on tiptoe she could now reach the top bolt and a few moments later she was opening the back door for the others to come in.

She smiled at Meg. She grinned at Art, who slapped her gently on the shoulder. She stuck her tongue out at Jonny. He glowered back, then his face crumpled into a smile and he stuck his tongue out back at her.

Art led them quietly toward the front of the warehouse. They made their way through the dusty corridors and across one of the huge machine rooms. The machinery had long since been removed, but the metal fittings and brackets still littered the floor and they picked their way with practiced care. As they neared the front of the room, Art held up his hand and they stopped.

In the distance ahead of them came the sound of movement, of voices. Flinch struggled to hear. She could make out broken snatches of conversation, shouted orders and questions, becoming clearer as they once again edged closer.

"Watch it, that's heavy . . ."

"Bring it around this end . . ."

"Where do you want this one, Professor?"

And a thin, reedy voice that carried distinctly through the air: "Be careful, Liza. We cannot afford any accidents at this stage."

It was apparent that the noises were coming from the next room, and they all crowded around Art as he edged the door open very slightly. Flinch, the smallest, had a good view from below, while the others jostled for position.

Where the back area had included machinery for packaging and sorting, the front of the warehouse had been storage space. Now the whole of this open area had been transformed. Partitions had sprung up, forming booths and small three-sided rooms. The result was that Flinch's view was limited.

But she could see clearly to the main loading area and

the road beyond. She could see the men carrying in more of the bodies draped in dustsheets. She bit back a gasp as one of the men stood a body upright and whipped off the sheet that covered it.

"This one?" His voice was a gruff bark.

"In the pub, for the moment," the thin reedy voice replied. A tall shadow stepped between Flinch and the body, close to the door. A silhouetted hand pointed the way, and Flinch could see that the tip of the man's middle finger was missing, stubbed off at the knuckle. "Be careful with it, the mechanism is especially delicate."

The gruff man lifted the body again and carried it away, letting the sheet lie where it had fallen. As he passed the door, Flinch and the others could clearly see what they had thought was a body.

It was a life-sized mannequin, shaped exactly like a man. It was clothed loosely in trousers and a grubby shirt. It seemed stiff and posed, one hand up where the mouth should be, little finger curled as if flicking at the lip. But there was no mouth, no lip. The face was a featureless blank of off-white. There was the hint of a bump where the nose might be, shadowed indentations that might one day be eyes, and the stubs of ears.

The man carried the featureless mannequin to one of the boarded-off areas. Flinch could just see inside and could make out that it did indeed look like a pub. A rough bar had been set up and there was shelving behind. Several more of the mannequins were propped up, as if ordering drinks from another mannequin that was standing upright behind the counter.

One of the men from the lorry was unpacking a small round table from a tea chest and arranging stools beside it. The gruff man stood his mannequin at the end of the bar, patted it on the shoulder, as if to tell it to stay where it was, and left for another load. The mannequin wobbled uncertainly for a moment.

"Liza," came the thin voice of the tall man, "check the mechanism on that one, would you?"

There was a shorter figure standing still and silent beside the mannequin. Flinch had taken it for another of the figures, but as she watched, it slowly turned and she saw that it was the girl from the cab. She had pushed back her hood and Flinch could see her face clearly. It was round and pale, framed by long, fine dark hair. Her eyes were large and china-blue. Her lips were full and very red. She looked about the same age as Art, or maybe a little older—perhaps fifteen, but no more.

The girl stumbled a step closer to the new mannequin, then reached up carefully and fiddled behind its head. When she was done, she stepped backward once more—again, an awkward movement. As she did so, her coat flapped open and Flinch could see the heavy frames of the metal braces that encased both her legs. She felt a moment of intense sadness for the girl.

Then the mannequin moved and the moment was gone.

Slowly, almost delicately, the mannequin completed the gesture it had frozen partway through. It wiped at its non-mouth with the curl of its little finger. So smooth and natural did the gesture seem that Flinch could imagine him wiping the froth from his mouth as he finished his pint of ale.

At that moment, the tall man stepped between the Cannoniers and the mannequin. He was talking with another man, a shorter man who stooped and coughed.

"I want it finished today," the tall man was saying.

"Yes, Professor," the other man said in a breathy voice. "Jake's putting the signs up now. All the apparatus is in and it's being unpacked."

"Good. We shall return later to check that everything is in order."

"It'll take a few days to get everything up and running proper," the smaller man wheezed.

"Of course it will," the professor snapped. "But I want the exhibition open for previews a week from today."

"Next Monday?" gasped the man in astonishment.

"At the latest."

The man shook his head in disbelief. "Monday," he repeated to himself, and turned to leave.

And as he turned, he looked straight at the doorway where Flinch and her friends were staring back at him. For a second he was framed in midturn. For a second she could see the men behind him raising a banner with writing on it, though she could not read what it said. For a second she was aware that the other alcoves and booths were also being dressed as exhibits—a prison cell here, a hotel lobby there, this one the bridge of a ship, that one the crypt of a church. Then the man was pointing, shouting, running in a shuffling, crouched manner toward them. And Art was dragging her back, calling to them all to run, and Jonny was already gone in a blur of motion.

They did not stop running until they were back on the other side of the street. The man had chased them as far as the machine room, but he soon caught his foot on a bracket or bolt, and gave up with a howl of rage and pain that brought a smile to Flinch's face.

"Professor Bessemer's Paranormal Puppets," Jonny said when they were safely hidden around the corner. He got his breath back before any of them, as usual. "That's what it said on that banner they were putting up."

"Yes," Art agreed. "It sounded like they were setting up a permanent exhibition of some sort."

"So we'll need another den," Meg said.

Art nodded sadly. "We will." He smiled at Flinch. "Never mind, Flinch, we'll find somewhere. There are plenty of empty factories around here. And we'll still be the Cannoniers, no matter what. But that's not what worries me."

Flinch believed him of course. She always believed Art. But she could see from his face that he was troubled. "What *does* worry you?" she asked.

He shook his head. "Probably nothing. Just a coincidence, I expect."

"What?" asked Meg. "You can tell us."

"I know." He thought for a moment, then gave a short laugh. "It was just that puppet, or whatever it was. The way it moved."

"Probably clockwork," Jonny said.

"What about it?" Meg asked.

"The way it wiped its mouth." Art demonstrated, mimicking the mannequin's movement with his hand.

"I thought it was funny," Flinch said. "Like he had beer on his moustache."

"That's right. Do you remember what Albert Norris said about Reggie Yarmouth—the man who's gone missing from his pub?"

Meg was staring at him as he spoke. "I remember," she said softly. "He said that Reggie had a funny way of wiping his mouth when he finished his pint."

"With his little finger curled up," Art added. "Like this." And he did the movement again. Exactly like Reggie Yarmouth. Exactly like the mannequin.

The second thing in the display case looked to Arthur like a piece of stone. It was only as the old man lifted it out and wiped the dust from its surface that he saw it was no ordinary pebble.

It was a flattened oval, and when the shopkeeper handed it to him, it fitted snug and warm in the palm of his hand. But it was the color that amazed him. It looked normal enough—a dull mixture of browns and greens—until it caught the light. Then it became an iridescent riot of bright, deep shades of blue, gold and red as well.

"What is it?" Arthur asked in wonder, the notebook he held in his other hand now forgotten.

"You don't know?" The old man's question seemed genuine and Arthur shook his head. "Neither do I," the shopkeeper admitted.

Arthur continued to stare at the strange stone, transfixed by the colors that escaped from its impossible depths. "How . . . ?" His voice seemed to catch in his throat.

"How much will I sell them for?"

"No. I meant, how did you get these? Where?"

But the shopkeeper ignored his words. "In a sense they are yours already, so I cannot ask you for too much. A pound, shall we say?"

"What?" Arthur looked up in surprise.

The old man's eyes were shining strangely. His glasses reflected the colored light from the stone. "Each," he added with a hint of amusement.

CHAPTER 4

They found an old storehouse on the corner of St. Swithin's Lane. Flinch had slept there a few times, so she knew how to work the loose bolt on one of the back doors. Some of the street children used to go there, she said, but not now. The floors were rotting and the fact that it had a frontage on Cannon Street meant that it was all too easy for the police to check it as they passed.

The last thing the warehouse had stored had been carpets. There were still huge rolls of decaying woolen material backed with canvas. In one of the storage areas they were piled up to more than three times Art's height. But when Jonny had started to scramble up the mountain of dusty rolls, his foot went through one and he tumbled down again, lucky not to break his leg.

"It's been here for years," Art said. "If it isn't rotted with the damp, then it's decayed with age." He slapped a roll next to him—almost as tall as he was. There was an explosion of dust and broken threads that made them all cough and laugh and cough again. The light that struggled through the dirty windows picked out the swirling particles as they drifted off into the shadows.

This was their new den. None of them ever said it, or asked the others for an opinion. It just *was*. As soon as Flinch led them inside, they all accepted the fact. They had exchanged the broken machinery and discarded metal brackets of their former meeting place for the dust-choked rolls of carpet and crumbling floors of a new one.

Again, they all agreed without a word that they would confine themselves to the ground floor. One look at the state of the galleries and rooms above, one step on any of the broken staircases that led up to the next level, was enough for them. Art was proud of them for that—they were just kids after all, he had no illusion there. But they were a team, they were friends, and they were all wise enough to know their limits.

Art was overconscious of his own limits. He might be the oldest, but his was the most sheltered of their lives. He didn't have the street experience of Flinch, or her knack of squeezing through the smallest of gaps. He envied Meg's ability to know instinctively when someone was lying—though he didn't envy the way she'd learned it, from her violent father and uncaring brothers. And Jonny could run—had to run—like no one else.

But the skill that Art had was one of leadership. Any of the others would have gone to the ends of the empire for him. Not because he told them what to do, but because of who and what he was. Art brought them all together and kept them together.

So, on the following Monday, when Art suggested that they go and see if the strange Professor Bessemer had yet opened his peculiar exhibition, there was no discussion or disagreement. If Art thought that was what they should do, then he was right. After all, Reggie Yarmouth had still not returned and the Invisible Detective was due to hold his next consulting session that very evening.

Jonny was keen that they should disguise themselves. "What if that creepy old man recognizes us?" he pleaded.

Meg glared at him. "Not very likely, is it?"

Jonny looked hurt. "But what if he does?" he insisted.

Art smiled gently. "It's a good thought," he said. "But I think Meg's right. It was pretty dark, and we were running away from him. Plus he's had a lot on his mind the last few days, getting the exhibition ready."

"I ain't got a disguise," Flinch said quietly, and Jonny dropped the idea.

Art was more concerned about whether they could afford the entrance fee. They had a little put away from the Invisible Detective's last few sessions, but that was to spend on Flinch. She would need a coat in the next few weeks. She had made herself a sort of nest out of the ragged ends of some of the better carpets, but that wouldn't be enough to keep the winter out.

The painted sign above the doors looked expensive and professional, and did nothing to ease Art's worries. PROFESSOR BESSEMER'S PARANORMAL PUPPETS, it proclaimed in block letters. And beneath that, italicized: *The Marvel of the Age*.

Art's heart lifted as he saw there was a chalkboard propped up outside the exhibition. Some of the letters were smudged and scuffed across to become ghostly shadows of themselves. But the text was clear enough: Today Only— Free Preview.

There were a few local people wandering around the exhibition. Most seemed impressed with the mechanisms that made many of the life-sized mannequins move, but, like Meg, they became bored before long and drifted away without completing the tour.

Meg's boredom was made worse by the fact that Jonny seemed entranced by the whole thing. Art, as ever, studied everything they saw in great detail. He nodded and clicked his tongue as if deducing the innermost secrets of Bessemer's techniques. Flinch walked through the whole thing with wide-eyed fascination.

But to Meg it seemed pointless. Each scene, each tableau, appeared to add very little to the previous ones. At first there was indeed something captivating about watching what she knew to be an artificial person go through a simple automatic routine. She watched a robed priest place a cardboard crown on the head of a blank-eyed queen. They were at the top of a huge flight of steps, the queen sitting, the priest standing beside her. But when the process was complete, the priest merely paused, then lifted the crown aloft once more, ready to go through exactly the same motions again. It was the same with the execution, with the torture cell, with the living room where a lonely old woman lifted an empty teacup to her pale face time after time. It reminded Meg of a story her mother had told her about a woman who measured out cloth from dawn till sunset after befriending a witch. Or had she drawn water from the well? It had been a long time ago. It was many years since Meg's mother had told her stories.

There was a small area painted green that was meant to be a park. An unconvincing view of a lake was daubed on the wall behind, and a moth-eaten dog bounced up and down as if trying to catch a ball that was strung from the wrist of a boy whose head was at an odd angle and whose legs were crooked.

By the time they got to the pub scene, Meg's boredom was ready to erupt. She was having trouble keeping still and her hands were balled into fists. She fought back her frustration while the others crowded as close as possible to the mannequin that seemed to wipe its mouth. A crude face had been affixed to the puppet's head and now he did indeed wipe at his moustache. Again and again.

Further along the bar, a pint was raised and lowered, raised and lowered. The barman polished a glass and it was only a matter of time, Meg decided, before he wore through it and started on his hands. Unless the cloth disintegrated first.

"Interesting," Art said.

Jonny nodded and Flinch remained transfixed.

"It is not interesting," Meg spat out. "Not remotely. Not even surprising."

"What do you mean?" Jonny asked, astonished at her outburst.

"I mean that out of the hundreds of puppets here, it is hardly a surprise that one of them makes a gesture that is similar to one made by someone else we've heard of. Not that any of us has ever seen it or can make a comparison," she finished.

The stiff figure behind the rope barrier in front of them wiped its moustache in apparent amusement at Meg's words.

"That's quite a good assessment," Art said. "I guess when we don't have any other clues, the slimmest of coincidences seems worth chasing."

"Talking of chasing," Jonny said in a low voice, "Old Creepy's back. Over there." He nodded across the exhibition.

The old man who had chased them the previous week was walking slowly, stiffly in their direction. His stoop seemed even more pronounced and his wrinkled face was twisted into a scowl of disapproval.

"Right," Art said quietly, "nobody say or do anything. He can't know for sure it's us. Just leave it to me if there's any trouble."

By now the man was almost level with them. He paused to watch one of the puppets in another display go through its routine, then turned and made his purposeful way toward the Cannoniers.

He stopped beside Flinch and glared at them, fixing each in turn with his cracked stare. Jonny smiled back nervously. Flinch edged away from the man. Meg did her best to remain impassive. Art seemed about to say something.

But the man spoke first. "Afternoon, kids," he said. "You

enjoying the show?" His eyes narrowed, seeming to retreat into his head as he waited for a reply.

"It's terrific," Art said. "Very impressive indeed."

The old man nodded, as if satisfied. But he made no sign of moving off.

"Great," Jonny said weakly.

"Interesting," Meg offered.

"I liked the dog," Flinch told him. As she spoke, her eyes widened. "Back in the little park. Trying to catch the ball that boy was throwing. There were ducks too," she added. "Painted on the back. On the lake."

The old man leaned down and ruffled Flinch's hair. Meg caught her breath in annoyance.

"I painted those ducks," the man whispered hoarsely. It sounded like a threat. Then he turned and walked away, leaving Flinch staring after him in apparent admiration.

"Don't let Mr. Crabtree upset you."

The soft voice startled Meg and she turned quickly. Beside her stood the girl from the cab, the girl they had seen helping set up the exhibition.

"I'm glad you find it interesting," she said to Meg. "Anton will be pleased—that's the professor." She blinked, and Meg saw that her lashes were long and dark, closing slowly over her moist eyes. "I'm Liza," she added.

"We're the Cannoniers," Flinch said.

Liza's expression did not alter. "Really?"

"This is Flinch," Art said. "I'm Art—Arthur Drake. This is Jonny and Meg."

"I'm very pleased to meet you," Liza replied. But from the way she was looking at Art, Meg doubted that they were all included.

"I expect you're busy," Meg said, "setting up the exhibition and everything." She forced a smile.

"It is a lot of work."

"I bet it is," Art enthused. "It's fascinating. Do the puppets work by clockwork, like an automaton, a robot?" He paused, as if he wasn't really sure what a "robot" was or why he had said it. Art did that sometimes. Meg had given up asking what he was talking about—he always just shrugged it off.

"Not quite."

But Meg cut her off. "We'd better be going," she said, "and leave you to your work."

"We're not in any hurry," Art said.

But Meg had his arm already. "Yes, we are," she said. "We still need to sort out what to say tonight."

"I suppose time is getting on," Jonny said.

They walked slowly to the doors. Slowly because Art kept trying to stop and look at the puppets, and slowly because Liza went with them. She had to walk carefully, lurching forward step by painful step. Without the long coat, the metal braces that supported her legs were clearly visible. Flinch seemed unable to look away from them, while Art was making an obvious point of not looking.

They were almost at the doors when Bessemer appeared and called Liza away. His thin voice echoed around the now almost empty exhibition.

Liza apologized for not seeing them out. "I hope we shall meet again soon," she said. Again, Meg noticed, she was addressing Art. "Just tell Anton or Mr. Crabtree or whoever is on the door, and they'll let you in free. As my guest."

"You're too kind," Meg said, stepping between the girl and Art.

Art's father cooked him tea. They sat opposite each other at the small kitchen table as they ate their bacon and scrambled eggs.

"Monday's your night with the gang, isn't it?" Peter Drake said. They both knew it was.

Art nodded, taking the cue. "Are you working tonight?" he asked.

"Hope not. But you can never tell these days."

"Is there a lot going on?"

"You could say that." Art's dad looked at him strangely, as if he was waiting for his son to ask more.

"Any missing persons?" Art asked casually as he wiped up the remains of the bacon fat with a piece of bread.

"As it happens, yes. Why do you ask?"

"Oh, nothing," Art said. "Only someone was saying that they hadn't seen old Reggie Yarmouth. Down at the Dog, you know." He shrugged and avoided catching his father's eye. "I just wondered. They seemed quite worried about him."

"Yes, well, Mr. Yarmouth is listed as missing," Peter Drake admitted. "But I don't know any more than that. Don't be too late back, will you?" For once there was an edge of anxiety in his voice.

"Don't worry, Dad." Art took his plate to the sink.

"I'll do the dishes. You get on and see your friends."

"Thanks."

Art's feelings were mixed as he got his coat. He had some information about Reggie Yarmouth. The Invisible Detective would again be able to reveal what was happening, however inconclusive that might be. But once more, Art was relying on his dad for the information. The others would want to know how he had found out, and there was no way he could tell them.

The Cannoniers were the best friends Art could ever have. He trusted them and they trusted him. Yet he continued to keep this one secret from them.

The knock at the door startled him. Art was reaching for the handle, lost in his thoughts, when the sound jolted him back to reality. He smiled at his own nervousness and opened the door. It stuck slightly just as it started to open— it always did when there was damp in the air.

There was a policeman standing outside, silhouetted against the late-afternoon sky. He bent forward toward Art. "Hello, young man," he said. "Your father around, is he?"

Art nodded in reply. His father: Detective Sergeant Peter Drake of Scotland Yard.

"It's for you, Dad," he called as he let the constable into the hallway.

Art's father was already there. The policeman stiffened respectfully.

"What is it, Wilkins?"

PC Wilkins glanced back at Art before he replied.

Taking the hint, Art gave his father a wave. "See you later," he said. He stepped outside and began to pull the door shut, slowly, straining to hear what Wilkins was saying behind him.

"They've found another one, sir." The constable's voice was low and confidential. "Down by the gasworks."

"Same as before?" Art heard his father ask.

"Yes, sir. It's a man's body, all right. Only . . ."

Art hesitated as the door almost reached the frame, struggling to catch the words from inside.

"Only—" PC Wilkins broke off, swallowed hard. "Only it's got no face, sir. Just a sort of bump of a nose, and dents for the eyes. . . ."

The rain had eased by the time Arthur made his way home. He walked slowly, thoughtfully, not noticing the puddles he

GYPSUM PUBLIC LIBRARY
P.O. BOX 979 • 48 LUNDGREN BLVD.
GYPSUM, CO 81637   (970) 524-5080

stepped in or the spray thrown up at him by the passing cars. In his hand he clutched the leather-bound notebook, while the colored pebble was heavy in his trouser pocket. He was not really sure why he had bought them, except that two pounds seemed like a good price.

And, of course, he was intrigued by the notebook that had his name and address and handwriting, yet was not his. The stone too interested him—it had an almost hypnotic quality that made it difficult to look away once you stared into its colorful depths.

It was after five by the time he got home. Arthur lived in a terraced house, faceless and bland. There was a short path from the gate through the paved front garden. His dad had to park on the street, but he wouldn't be home till after six. Time enough to get the tea ready.

The front door stuck as he pushed it open. It always did after the rain—the wood swelled with the damp, Dad said. One day he might get around to fixing it.

Arthur put the notebook and the stone on his bedside cabinet and went back downstairs to check the fridge. In his mind, he was already going through a list of questions he meant to ask Dad. Questions about his family, about the house. He could remember moving in about six years before, when he was eight. So how could someone called Arthur Drake have lived there nearly seventy years ago? Was it a joke? Maybe the book was something Dad had done for a laugh. But that didn't seem likely.

He'd ask his dad when he got home, while they were having tea. And when Dad was evasive, or just didn't know, Arthur would say what he always said, all mock-innocent and serious, "But you *must* know, Dad. You're a policeman."

CHAPTER 5

The evening was already drawing in. Dull clouds gathered and there was a hint of moisture in the air. Jonny turned up the collar of his coat and sank his chin down so that it was pressed into his neck. But that was not because of the chill of the quickening breeze. Jonny was in disguise.

"She'd be worth keeping an eye on," Art had said as they left the strange exhibition.

Jonny could remember the bite of disapproval in Meg's tone. "Oh, yes?" she had replied.

But Art seemed not to notice it. "Yes," he'd said, nodding thoughtfully. "How about it, Jonny?"

Which was why Jonny was missing the consulting session, why he was keeping to the shadowy side of the street, and why he was following the young girl as she made her slow, lurching way from the exhibition. The clock outside the jeweler's told Jonny that he had half an hour until he was supposed to meet Art and report anything of interest. Not that Art would mind if he was late, or if he was still watching Liza. They'd meet at the new den tomorrow after school whatever happened.

For the moment, though, Jonny was inclined to agree with Meg. There seemed little point in following Liza. Maybe he should head back to the locksmith's and catch the end of the Invisible Detective's consulting session. Having come to a decision, Jonny was about to turn around, but then he stopped.

Ahead of him the girl was already crossing the road. And Jonny could tell from her purposeful manner as she stumbled onward where she was headed. On the corner in front of them was a pub—the Dog and Goose. The sign was swinging gently in the wind, squeaking for want of oil. The image on it was cracked and faded—a small terrier drawing back in surprise from a large goose that was jabbing at it with her beak.

Probably it was a coincidence. The Dog was the closest pub to the exhibition after all. But that the mysterious Professor Bessemer's assistant, or whatever she was, should visit the very place from which Reggie Yarmouth had gone missing seemed worth investigating. So Jonny followed Liza across the road and into the pub.

It seemed darker inside than out. The wooden floor was stained with spilled drinks and littered with cigarette ends. The air was swirling with smog. The smell of tobacco, beer and sweat made Jonny catch his breath. The pub was crowded, and he had to force his way through the mass of bodies toward the bar. He did not want a drink, of course, but he was struggling to keep Liza within sight. Despite her small, frail form, she made quick progress as the people drew back to allow her through, before closing ranks again as if deliberately trying to slow Jonny's own progress.

Eventually he managed to get to a point from where he

could see Liza while remaining inconspicuous. She was standing at the bar, her head turning as if she was looking for someone. As she turned in his direction, Jonny looked away to hide his face. He was hot, could feel his face glowing with embarrassment and nerves. When he dared to look back, it was in time to see a young, sandy-haired man push his way along the bar until he was next to Liza.

She was facing away from Jonny, so he could not see her reaction, but the man's face was earnest and serious. His eyes were wide and unblinking as he spoke to her. His nose was crooked in the middle where it had been broken and not mended properly. Liza stepped awkwardly away from the bar. Immediately the young man grabbed her wrist, pulling her back. Then he waved to the barman and shouted for ale.

Jonny took a step toward them, unsure what to do. The man was heavily built and the muscles stood out on his bare arms. If he wanted to talk to Liza, there was not a lot that Jonny—or Liza—would be able to do to stop him. Jonny hesitated, glanced at the clock above the bar, then began to push his way back through the mass of people toward the door.

"Is Mr. Norris with us this evening?" the Invisible Detective asked.

"Yes, sir—here, sir," Norris replied. He shuffled nervously. "Reggie ain't been back, sir," he added.

"Yes, I know." There was a pause, then Brandon Lake continued: "An unfortunate business."

"You know what's happened to him, sir?" Norris asked hopefully.

"I am afraid not," the detective admitted. There was a collective sigh of disappointment from the people in the room. "But . . ." Immediately there was silence again. "But I can reveal to you that Scotland Yard has Reggie Yarmouth listed officially as a missing person." Several audible gasps at this news. "So, Mr. Norris, your fears are well founded. And I thank you for bringing the matter to my attention. And indeed to the attention of the police."

Of course, Art thought as he sat facing the window, the Invisible Detective had not brought the matter of Reggie Yarmouth's disappearance to the attention of the police. They already knew about it. But it did no harm to imply a connection between Norris's query and the investigation. And it wouldn't do Brandon Lake's reputation any harm either.

"I shall of course furnish you with whatever news is forthcoming as soon as it breaks," Art went on.

It was muggy and close in the room this evening, as if there was going to be a storm. Art would be glad to get finished, and he was looking forward to talking to Jonny about whether Liza had left the exhibition and, if so, where she had gone. There was something about the girl that intrigued him. Something about her delicate features, her large eyes, her vulnerability. He wouldn't dare mention it to the others—especially not Meg—but Art was worried about her.

He did not believe for an instant that she was in any way involved in the disappearances, but he was concerned about Bessemer. If he was implicated, then Liza could be in danger. For a moment Art could see the two of them in his mind's eye—Bessemer looming over the frightened girl like a movie villain, and Liza desperately trying to back away, to escape, hampered by her damaged legs. What had happened to them, he wondered. An accident? Or had she been born crippled, had her legs simply never developed properly?

"I think that concludes our business for this evening," Art heard himself saying in his deepest voice. "There is just time to take questions ready for our next consulting session, then I must bid you good evening."

Jonny was waiting for them outside, on the other side of the road. He was kicking his feet nervously and ran across to Art as soon as he and the girls emerged from the locksmith's.

"How did it go?" Jonny asked. But it was obvious to Art that he had something else on his mind.

"Fine. And you?"

"I followed the girl, Liza, like you said."

Meg clicked her tongue in annoyance. "Waste of time," she grumbled.

"Art," Jonny went on urgently, "she went to the Dog and Goose. That's where Reggie Yarmouth disappeared from."

"No, it isn't," Meg chided him. "It's somewhere he used to go. Anyway, it's the nearest pub to the exhibition, so it means nothing."

Jonny was looking appealingly at Art.

Art shrugged. "Meg's right," he admitted.

"P'raps she wanted a drink," Flinch offered diffidently. "She's old enough, ain't she?"

"Old enough to know better," Meg said. "And so are you, Arthur Drake."

Art sighed. She only called him "Arthur" when she was annoyed. "It was just an idea," he said. "We don't exactly have hundreds of leads in this case."

"If it is a case." Meg glared at Jonny. "What is it now?"

The boy was almost hopping up and down, desperate to speak. "I think she might be in trouble," he said. "She was talking to this man. At the bar. Only . . . Only I didn't like the look of him." He shrugged, as if unable to put into words what his anxiety really was.

Meg nodded in apparent satisfaction. "Talking to a man at the bar," she said quietly. "Well maybe she went there to meet him. Or someone. Art?"

Art nodded. "Maybe." But he was worried by Jonny's evident anxiety. "Perhaps we'd better check she's all right. You know. Just in case."

Meg was staring at him. "I have to get home," she said.

"Come on, Flinch. I'll walk back to the den with you on the way."

"Good-bye, Art. Jonny," Flinch called over her shoulder as Meg led her away. "See you tomorrow."

"Sure," Art said.

"Yes, right. Bye," Jonny called.

"Good-bye, Jonny," Meg called back. She did not turn around.

It was beginning to rain as they reached the Dog and Goose. Large drops splashed heavily into growing puddles. Art blinked the water from his eyes and wiped at his damp hair. For the briefest moment he thought he could remember standing outside the locksmith's in the rain.

Except it wasn't a locksmith's now. The windows were dusty and beyond them the room was the same, but filled with all manner of bits and pieces—books and ornaments, tables and other furniture—rather than Mr. Jerrickson's workbench and the hooks loaded with key blanks.

But then the impression—the memory, if that's what it was—had gone and he was staring at Jonny and watching the water dripping off the end of his nose.

"I said, 'Are we going inside?' "

Art was about to answer when the door of the pub was shoved open and two figures staggered out. One was staggering from the effects of too much drink. The other Art recognized at once as Liza, despite the heavy coat she wore and the hood that concealed her face in shadow. The fair-haired man was holding Liza by the arm. But as they lurched down the few steps from the door to the pavement, it was difficult to tell if he was holding on for support or to stop her from getting away from him.

Jonny took a step toward the figures now standing before them in the rain, but Art caught him by the shoulder and held him back.

The two figures—one tall but stooping, the other short but upright—took several difficult steps toward Art and Jonny. Then, as they watched through the slanting rain, the girl pulled her arm away from the man's grasp and hurried in her halting, rolling manner ahead of him.

The man paused, as if confused. Then he started after her. She glanced back, to see if he was following, braced foot splashing into a puddle and sending up a spray of dirty droplets. The man was staggering, lurching after her. Art could see that his face was set, expressionless, a mask of concentration. He meant to catch up with her.

"Come on," Art said. The wind was whipping at their hair in the darkening evening. The rain beat an insistent, staccato rhythm on the pavement. "You help Liza." It was raining bats and frogs now—where had he heard a phrase like that? Art couldn't recall anyone saying it, but it was familiar nonetheless.

Jonny ran to help Liza stagger more quickly away from the man. Art grinned at them as he ran past, his hand up at his face to conceal his features. The man might be drunk, but Art didn't want to risk him remembering the face of the boy who collided with him on a wet evening and sent him flying.

He dropped his shoulder as he ran at the man, felt it jab into his ribs, caught a glimpse of a confused face with a crooked nose. Art staggered on. "Sorry, mate," he called in a broad cockney accent as he kept running. When he reached the next corner, he turned and crossed the road before running back on the other side of the street. The man was struggling to pull himself up out of a puddle, shaking water from his hands and staring down in disbelief at his drenched clothing.

Art caught up with Jonny and Liza further along the street. "Are you all right?" He had to shout above the wind and the rain. He knew he was grinning, but somehow he couldn't help it.

"Fine, thank you." The girl's words seemed to carry easily to him. "Really," Liza assured him, and Art realized he had been staring at her.

"Sorry," he mumbled. "Looked like you needed some help."

"You were at the exhibition," she said. The light from a nearby window was shining into the hood so that Art could see her face, could see the large blue eyes that were fixed on him. "You will come back and see us again, won't you?"

"Us?" Art said. He meant himself and Jonny.

But she misunderstood. "Me," she said. "Come and see me." Her expression did not change, but he could hear the warmth in her voice, felt almost compelled by it.

"Of course we will," Jonny said. "Thanks."

But the girl was still looking at Art. "I have to get back," she said. "I can manage now. Thank you." Then she turned and made her ponderous way along the pavement.

Art and Jonny stood watching her. Neither spoke for several minutes as the rain ran in little rivers down their faces and coats.

"See you tomorrow, then," Jonny said at last.

"Yes," Art said. "Tomorrow." But when he looked around, Jonny had already gone.

The man who had left the pub with Liza stood as if in a daze. His clothes were soaked through and he was shivering with the cold. But he seemed not to notice. He staggered forward, stumbling through puddles, quickening his pace. Before long he was running, an uncertain, ungainly movement along the pavement.

He was in time to see Liza arrive at the front of the warehouse that was now the home of Professor Bessemer's Paranormal Puppets. He skidded to a halt as she opened the small door in the main gates, turned for a brief moment and stared back at him. Her eyes locked with his for just a second. Then she turned away and stepped inside. The door closed and he was left alone in the rain.

How long he stood there he never knew, but after a while a car drew up beside him. Large and black, it glistened wet in the lamplight, its headlights illuminating the warehouse doors. The driver reached over the seat and opened the back door behind him. It almost brushed the man's soaking coat as it swung past him. The driver's window was open and his hand beckoned for the man to get in—a hand on which the middle finger was a short stump of flesh and bone.

Slowly, as if in a daze, the man bent down and climbed into the car. He closed the door behind him and the driver wound up his window. Had he turned, the man would have seen a third figure, seated beside him in the back of the car. Had he looked at the figure's clothes, he would have noticed that they were remarkably like his own—a dark jacket over a white shirt, faded cotton trousers, boots that had seen better days. If he had chanced to examine the figure's face, he would have seen nothing but a pale, blank oval. Dents where there should have been eyes and a slight bump for the nose.

But the man was staring sightlessly ahead as the car pulled away and drove off into the night.

"Is this a project for school?" Arthur's dad asked him.

"Something like that." Arthur shifted uncomfortably in his chair. "We were talking about family histories, home and stuff. I was just interested."

They had finished tea, but they were both still sitting at

the kitchen table. Arthur's dad got to his feet and carried the dirty plates over to the sink.

"Well, this is as close as we have to a family home, I suppose."

"I remember moving here," Arthur said. "So it can't have been that long ago."

"That's true. But I lived here as a boy."

Arthur frowned. "How come?"

"You don't remember?" Dad seemed amused. "I guess you were very young." He returned to the table and sat down again. "This was your grandad's house. My house, before I moved out and got married. Then Grandad moved into Wingate Manor, and you and I came back here."

"Where were we before that?"

"Not far away." Dad stared off into the distance. "A bigger place. We thought, your mother and I, that we'd need the space. But it turned out we didn't. When your mother—" He broke off and stood up again. "Anyway," he went on, running the tap with his finger in the stream of water as he waited for it to get hot, "we needed somewhere a bit cheaper. Smaller." He half turned back toward Arthur, trying to smile. "And, like I said, it's our family home. There have been Drakes here for over a hundred years." The water was hot now and he held the plates under the jet, wiping halfheartedly with a cloth. "Some of them quite famous."

"Really?" Arthur joined his dad at the sink. He grabbed a tea towel off the hook and started to dry the plates. There was still a sheen of grease on one of them, but he said nothing.

"Arthur," his dad said quietly. "Now there's a good family name for you."

"Dad?" he asked hesitantly, not sure if he should say it or not.

"Mmm?"

"Have you ever heard of the Invisible Detective?" He looked sideways at his dad, angling his eyes so he seemed not to be paying too much attention.

"Of course I have."

Arthur nearly dropped the fork he was drying. "Really?"

"Yes. It's that new TV thing, isn't it?" He wrung out the cloth and dropped it behind the tap. "Or is that *The Invisible Dog*? Why do you ask?"

"Nothing, Dad." Arthur smiled thinly. "It's not important."

CHAPTER 6

Dawn was breaking over the Thames. The sunlight rippled on the water, taking the edge off the chilly morning. Already London was waking up, and Alan Wilkins could hear the city coming to life. He pulled his cape tighter around his neck and gestured to the man with the boat hook.

"Easy with that now. See if you can hook his collar. We don't want you stabbing the poor chap."

"Righto, Constable." The man was one of the stevedores from the docks further down. He walked to work along the riverbank, picking his way across the mudflats, no doubt looking for anything valuable that might have washed up. There was something washed up this morning. That was what had sent the man running toward Monument, where he had found Wilkins.

The body was half-submerged in the oily water, face down. They had taken so long trying to catch it with the boat hook as it dipped and turned, there was no chance the man was still alive.

At last the hook caught in the collar of the dead man's dark jacket, pulling it forward over his head as the body bobbed toward the bank. Wilkins could see a sodden white shirt hanging out of faded cotton trousers. A single boot broke the surface as the head dipped and the legs pivoted up—a boot that had seen better days. The other foot was bare, pale and slicked with muck.

It took them several more minutes to drag the body to the bank, both of them heaving on the boat hook. Eventually, between them, they managed to drag the waterlogged corpse out of the river. It flopped on the mud, arms stretched out as if trying to swim awkwardly. The smell of the river caught in Wilkins's throat and made him gag as he stooped and rolled the body over.

The sun was shining directly on the corpse's face as it turned, bleaching the features with cold, early-morning light. Wilkins straightened up and nodded grimly. There was no satisfaction in the movement, only resignation.

"Oh, my good Lord." The stevedore crossed himself, swallowing hard.

"You found a body," Wilkins told him. "That's all. If anyone asks, or you want to tell them, that's it. Just a body." He fixed his gaze on the man's frightened eyes and hoped he seemed calm and in control. "Nothing more. Some poor chap who fell in and was drowned."

The docker shook his head. The boat hook was lying forgotten in the mud as he backed away. "I seen some things," he muttered, "seen what the water can do to a man . . . But I ain't . . ." He crossed himself again. "I ain't never seen nothing like that. Not ever."

He turned and ran, his feet sticking and squelching in the mud as he struggled to put as much distance as he could between himself and the river; between himself and PC Wilkins; between himself and the faceless corpse lying on the bank as the sun dried the mud around it.

Art had not slept well. He'd had strange dreams. They seemed to make no sense, filled with people and things he half remembered. But as he woke, with the morning sun angling through his window and shining across his face, the dreams fled.

His father was already gone. A hurried note on the kitchen table told him to make his own breakfast, but he wasn't hungry. So he left early, deciding to look in on Flinch at the new den on his way to school.

It wasn't really on his way, but he had plenty of time. The streets were already busy with people going to work as he approached the warehouse. Somewhere down by the river he could hear a police whistle—insistent bursts of shrill sound. He turned to try to work out where it was coming from.

As he turned, he caught his foot on the uneven pavement and stumbled. He regained his balance immediately, but his shoulder knocked into the side of a man walking past him. The man was well dressed in a dark, newly pressed suit. A mass of white hair erupted from beneath his top hat and his pale eyes were wide with surprise as he staggered under the impact. Art quickly caught the man by the shoulder, apologizing.

"I'm sorry—I caught my foot. Are you all right?"

"I'm fine, thank you." The man had recovered his composure as well as his balance and he regarded Art with a twinkle of amusement. "You should watch where you're going, young man."

"Yes, sir, I'm sorry," Art said again.

"Lost in your thoughts, in a world of your own."

"Well . . ." Art smiled sheepishly and made to walk away.

"No harm in that." The man's voice seemed to hold him back. He couldn't just walk off, not while the man was talking to him. "I've seen you around here before, haven't I? You and your young friends."

The man smiled again at Art's embarrassment. "Don't worry," he said, laughing now. "It's nice to see youngsters enjoying themselves." He leaned forward, as if about to impart a huge secret. "You may not believe this," he said quietly, eyes flicking from side to side as if to check they were not being overheard, "but I was young myself once."

Art laughed too at this. "I'm sorry I knocked into you," he said.

"That's quite all right." The man turned, and Art thought he was about to walk away, but instead he pointed at the warehouse—at the Cannoniers' new den. "When I was young, I remember that warehouse being built."

"Really?"

"Now it's broken down and decayed. Past its prime. A bit like me, I suppose." He nodded slowly before turning back to Art. "Still makes a pretty good den, though, I expect."

Art blinked. "Sorry?"

"Saw you and your friends coming out the other day. I walk along here every morning and back again most evenings, you know."

Art looked at the man more closely. His face was wrinkled, but it was not as ancient as he had first thought. His voice was kindly enough and his eyes were alive with intelligence and humor. "No doubt I'll see you again," the man said. He paused. "I'm sorry, I don't know your name."

"Arthur," Art said. "Art for short." It was an automatic response.

"Art," the man repeated. "Well, I'm pleased to meet you, Art. My name is Charles. Call me Charlie for short, although it isn't really shorter."

"How do you do?" Art said. It sounded a bit lame.

"Do something for me, Art," the man said, his expression suddenly serious.

"If I can."

"Be careful in there," the man—Charlie—said. "And tell your friends. The floors will be rotten and the roof's none too good, I'm sure. It's easy to get carried away when you're young, when you're playing. I remember." He smiled again. "Now, if you'll excuse me. It was nice bumping into you."

The elderly man tipped his hat politely to Art, then turned and strode purposefully away down Cannon Street.

Art watched him disappear, swallowed up by the crowd on the pavement.

The office where Detective Sergeant Peter Drake worked was just slightly too small to be comfortable. His desk was also just too small for the amount of paperwork he had piled on it. An exposed, cramped area of blotter was left for him to work on in among the clutter.

"In already, Drake?" announced a booming voice, startling him. "Good man." Inspector Mervyn Gilbertson was a huge figure who almost filled the office doorway, blotting out the light from the corridor. "Found another faceless body this morning, I hear. Down in the river." He shook his head. "Be hell to pay when Fotherington gets his nose into the files."

"Lord Fotherington, sir?" Drake had met Fotherington. He was a thorough but fair man.

Gilbertson nodded unhappily. "He's been charged with making some sort of report on the state of policing in London. For the home secretary, no less. So he'll be talking to you about your faceless bodies and your missing persons."

Drake nodded slowly. As if things were not bad enough already.

Gilbertson seemed to read his thoughts. He sucked in his cheeks, making his whiskers quiver. "I don't know," he mused. "What a week. Already we've got another one of these bodies, my superiors are getting all hot under the collar, my wife's talking about getting her ears pierced and, to top it all, Lord Fotherington's coming in to sort us out. What more do we need?"

Drake laughed. "The Invisible Detective?" he suggested.

Gilbertson frowned. "The what?"

"Oh, nothing, sir. Some nonsense on my patch. This chap calls himself the Invisible Detective. Sits in a darkened room and finds lost cats and wandering children. That sort of thing. The locals are impressed." He shrugged. "At the moment I think I'd welcome any sort of help."

"Yes," Gilbertson said quietly. "Well, let's not get too carried away, shall we?" He turned to leave. "Let me have a report when you get a chance. I'd like to be up to date on how awful things are."

Inspector Gilbertson's office was considerably larger than Drake's. The inspector settled himself massively into the swivel chair behind his desk and drummed his fingers on the blotter as he thought. "Victoria," he called loudly through the open door.

A moment later his secretary was standing in the doorway, notebook in hand. She was a middle-aged woman, as thin and efficient as her poised pencil. Her hair was tied into a tight bun and she wore horn-rimmed spectacles that, together with her severe expression, made her look older than she really was. "Fotherington here yet?" Gilbertson demanded.

"Not yet, sir. You're due to see him at ten o'clock."

Gilbertson nodded. "I know. Thank you, Victoria. Oh, one other thing," he added as she turned to go.

"Sir?"

"Ask around and see what you can find out about some chap in the Cannon Street area, would you? Apparently he calls himself the Invisible Detective."

If Arthur's father thought it was odd that his son headed up to bed so early, he said nothing. Arthur often read late into the night. Usually he curled up on the sofa, half aware of his father watching the television and grateful for the company.

But tonight he wanted to be alone. Once in his pajamas, he got into bed and wriggled his back against the pillow until he was comfortable. Then he opened the leather-bound notebook and began to read.

It took him a while to get into it. The handwriting was familiar—it was his own handwriting—so he had no trouble deciphering the hurried scrawl. But much of it was written in the form of short notes, making it difficult to follow. There were accounts of meetings that seemed to be question-and-answer sessions. But the answers often came in dribs and drabs, well after the questions were posed.

There was a long description of someone called Flinch crawling through a wall to find a boy who had fallen into a drain. Later there was an account of a visit to some sort of waxworks exhibition. Except that the figures were animated with a mechanism. It all sounded a bit advanced for the 1930s.

Rather more unsettling, when he stopped to consider it, Arthur found that he had no trouble visualizing the events and things that were mentioned. Nowhere was there a description of the "consulting sessions," yet he could see the darkened room without any conscious effort to imagine it. He could hear the people chattering, shuffling, asking questions. He knew, although it was never stated, that there were people behind the curtains. One of them he felt sure was holding a fishing rod. He could see Flinch and Meg and Jonny as clearly as if he went to school with them.

"This is just so weird," Arthur muttered to himself as he turned another page and stared at the spidery writing.

I'm having weird dreams was scrawled across the bottom of the page, the writing bigger and somehow more urgent than the other notes. *Like I'm someone else, somewhere else.*

The last words were angled so they ran up the edge of the page when whoever wrote them ran out of space at the bottom. Arthur turned the book to follow them.

But it's like I'm dreaming things I'd forgotten rather than things I never knew.

As he turned the book upright again, Arthur glimpsed something moving out of the corner of his eye. He looked quickly across at his bedside cabinet. But it was just the light catching the surface of the strange pebble he had bought from the antiques shop. He picked it up, looking again into the depths of light and color.

After a few minutes, the notebook slipped from Arthur's other hand, falling and closing on the bed covers. His eyelids fluttered like a butterfly's wings and Arthur Drake began to dream.

CHAPTER 7

The weekends were better for Flinch. The others were not in school and they brought her food. During the week, when the others weren't around, she had to scavenge if she got hungry. She didn't like to ask or beg from strangers, but she could often find scraps of food around the back of the tearooms up by the Monument.

The weekends were better for Jonny. He didn't have to hide in the corner of the playground between lessons, or ignore the comments and names from Alf Bickerstaff and his mates. He rarely had a nosebleed at the weekend, hardly ever ran home to crawl shivering into the space between his bed and the wall.

The weekends were worse for Meg. Her father got home later on weekends, but he invariably woke Meg as he stumbled up the stairs, or snored in the armchair, or shouted at Meg's mother. In the mornings Meg was torn between leaving before her father woke up and staying to see if her mother was all right. Since her brothers had left home, there were just the three of them. On the weekends in particular, Meg and her mother collected bruises.

Art was happy at school, keeping himself to himself, updating his casebook and reading in every spare moment. On the weekends he relished the time he could spend with the Cannoniers. It had been his decision to hold the Invisible Detective's weekly consulting sessions on a Monday evening. It lifted Jonny and Flinch from the depression brought on by the start of another week. It helped Meg to get through the weekend knowing that Monday evening was almost upon them. It gave the gang a whole week to think about how best to spend the next weekend solving the problems put to the Invisible Detective.

Monday evenings were exciting, they were fun and, despite the constant thrill at the prospect of discovery, they were safe. There was no chance now that anyone would discover the real identity of Brandon Lake. Art had the sessions organized into a standard routine. Together they were in control, able to deal with whatever happened above the locksmith's on a Monday evening.

Or so they all thought.

The sunlight angled dustily through the gap in the curtains. Jonny stood watching the vague outline of Brandon Lake in the armchair. Flinch was close beside him, her face alight with happiness and friendship. Meg, for once, was at the back of the room, playing the part of an interested kid, there to hear what went on. Art was putting on his usual incredible performance, though his voice sounded a little husky. Perhaps the dust was getting to him, Jonny thought.

The session was drawing to a close. The Invisible Detective had put Mrs. Dawson's mind at rest about the man selling encyclopedias who really did work for Offcut Publishers. Harris Matthews now knew the going rate for the sort of insurance he wanted. Everyone was relieved that the rumors of doping at the dog track were unfounded, or at least no more founded than usual.

Jonny could hear the impatient shuffling of feet that heralded the end of the session. A few more words from Brandon Lake—his "summing up," as Art called it—and another consulting session would be over.

But in among the shuffling, Jonny could hear another sound. A steady, heavy beat that was slowly growing in volume. The other noises in the room seemed to die away even as it grew louder. Someone was walking up the stairs. Someone with heavy feet, confidence and a purpose.

"Sounds like Old Bill himself," someone close to the curtain muttered.

They were quickly shushed.

Jonny and Flinch both shifted position to try to see the top of the stairs. Across the room, Meg looked over at them, her eyes full of warning, before she too turned to see who was coming.

"Looks as though I've come to the right place." The voice boomed around the now silent room. A large silhouette stepped out of the stairwell and paused. "Don't let me interrupt, please. You all carry on."

When the Invisible Detective spoke, his voice was slightly more nasal and high-pitched than usual.

"I think that concludes our consultation for today. If anyone has anything else to ask, now is your last opportunity until next Monday evening."

There was a general movement toward the stairs. People picked their way around the newcomer, giving the large figure plenty of room.

"I have a question," the man announced in his parade-ground voice. He stepped forward, a path opening up effortlessly through the people still in the room. "A question I wish to ask in private," he said, his voice slightly lowered now.

"May I ask your name, sir?"

The man gave a snort of amusement. "I think some of the people here know who I am," he said. "But if it will help to speed the others on their way about their business . . ."

He paused to look around the gloomy room. Jonny and Flinch both stepped back behind the curtains as the man's bewhiskered face caught the light.

"My name," he said, "is Gilbertson. Inspector Gilbertson of Scotland Yard."

Meg followed the other people as they made their way past Gilbertson and down the stairs. But when she reached the top of the stairs she hesitated and glanced back at the large man standing in the middle of the room. His attention seemed to be fixed entirely on the back of the faded armchair. Meg waited for the last few people to pass, then slipped silently behind the curtains and edged along until she was standing with Jonny and Flinch.

Jonny was staring through the narrow gap between the curtains. She could see him chewing nervously at his lower lip. Flinch grinned at Meg. She was excited, shifting her weight from one foot to the other as they all strained to hear what was going on.

There was no problem hearing Gilbertson when he spoke. His voice echoed around the room. "I'm sure you've heard," he said, "about the people who've gone missing in the area. Not many, true. But enough to have us worried."

"Indeed." For the first time, Meg wondered how anyone could fail to realize that Brandon Lake's voice was really that of a boy speaking slowly and deeply.

"You may also know that we've found several bodies."

"That has not escaped my attention."

"Good." Gilbertson paused, as if considering whether to say anything more.

Jonny's lips were moving impatiently. "Come on, come on," Meg imagined him muttering.

Eventually, Gilbertson did go on. He spoke slowly, almost cautiously. "What you won't know is that there is something rather odd about those bodies. That's why we can't be sure they are the people reported as missing. You see . . ."

The detective's deep voice interrupted him: "The bodies," he said, "have no face. Just a bump of a nose, and dents where there should be eyes."

Even behind the curtain, Meg heard the man catch his breath. "How did you . . . ?" His voice tailed off. "I'm impressed," he went on a moment later. "Perhaps I really have come to the right place."

"You want my help?" the Invisible Detective asked.

"You have come to the point where you have no other leads, nothing else to go on. You're desperate."

"I was going to phrase it more tactfully," Gilbertson admitted, "but yes. That's about the size of it. Anything you might know, might hear. I believe that you can get information from the locals more easily and readily than my men could. Not that they don't trust us, but you seem to be accepted as part of the community, as an expert, someone who helps."

Meg was holding her breath. Part of her was desperate for Art to agree to help. But another part of her dreaded the idea of being caught up in something this serious—this *real*. It might be exciting, but it could be dangerous. This wasn't like finding a lost dog or asking after Reggie Yarmouth. This was a police matter. Maybe murder. Maybe worse, though she wasn't really sure what could be worse.

"I can make no promises," the detective said at last. "But I shall do what I can and report back to you at the earliest opportunity."

"I'm very grateful." Gilbertson sounded relieved. "Just one other thing."

"Yes?"

"You won't be reporting back to me. I came here on a whim really, but now I'm sure it was the right thing to do. So you'll hand over whatever information you can to the officer in charge of the case."

"Very well."

"I imagine he'll want to meet you in person. None of

this hugger-mugger darkened rooms and shadows business. Face-to-face, so the two of you can discuss matters properly and sort out a strategy of how to deal with . . . whatever's going on."

Art did not answer. Meg could imagine his mind racing through the possibilities and problems this raised.

Gilbertson seemed to take the silence for agreement. "Good," he said. "Well, I'll be on my way. I'll leave my card with the sixpences on the table here. I've written my man's name and details on the back for you."

Meg could hear the inspector's heavy footsteps as he made his way purposefully back toward the stairs. As soon as he was gone, she ran to the table and picked up the business card. The top left corner was bent, she noticed, as she turned it over to see what was written on the back. There was a phone number and then a name. She read it out: "Detective Sergeant Peter Drake."

Art said nothing on the journey back to the new den. The others were talking quietly among themselves, but his mind was a fog and he could hardly make out their words. The dust from the rolls of carpet hung in the air around them as he sat down glumly on the tattered remains of something with a paisley pattern. He rubbed his forehead and wondered how he had come to this. What should he say?

"It's all right, Art," Meg said gently. She sat down beside him. Jonny and Flinch watched anxiously. "We'll work something out. Maybe you won't have to meet him."

Art looked up at her, grateful for her concern. "You don't understand," he told her, aware of the tension in his voice. "It isn't just a coincidence. The name, I mean."

"Detective Sergeant Peter Drake?" Meg asked.

He nodded and looked away.

"He's your dad," Flinch said.

"Flinch!" Meg snapped at her, and the girl looked away.

"How did you guess?" Art asked. At least he was saved the humiliation of telling them.

"She didn't guess," Jonny said. "She knew."

"What?"

"We all knew," Meg said quietly. "We've always known. Well, for a long time anyway."

"That's how you find stuff out," Flinch said. She was smiling again. "From your dad, the policeman."

"You knew?" Art couldn't believe this. "But—why didn't you say?"

Jonny shrugged. "You didn't want to tell us. That's your business."

"I thought . . ." Art sighed and shook his head. "I don't know what I thought. But I didn't want to lose you all. Leave the Cannoniers."

"Because of your dad?" Meg said. She slapped him on the shoulder. "It isn't your dad who's in the Cannoniers, is it?"

"Least you've got a dad," Flinch said quietly. She flopped down on the floor, pulling her legs under her and gazing down at the dusty boards.

"And just look at *my* dad," Meg said. She was half smiling, but her voice was sad. "You've got nothing to be ashamed of."

Jonny shuffled his feet awkwardly. "So what do we do, then?" he asked. "Art?"

Art took a deep breath. He still felt cold and empty inside, surprised and at the same time almost elated. They knew, and the world hadn't ended, he wasn't banished from the den. They were still looking to him for guidance.

"Well, it's obvious I can't go to my dad and tell him I'm the Invisible Detective."

"Why not?" Flinch said, rubbing fiercely at her eyes and sniffing noisily.

"I don't think he'd believe me, for one thing," Art told her gently. "And for another, we'd be off the case. Scotland Yard might consider calling in the mysterious Brandon Lake, but they wouldn't ask for help from a bunch of kids." He smiled, as best he could. "Even us."

"So what's the plan?" Jonny asked again.

Art sighed. "I think we have to bow out gracefully."

"What do you mean?" Meg asked severely.

"I mean we send a message to the Yard—to my dad or Gilbertson—and say that the Invisible Detective is sorry but he's found out nothing." Art looked around at their disappointed faces. "Well, it's true," he said.

"No, it isn't," Meg told him. "There's Reggie Yarmouth's puppet or whatever it is."

"That's hardly—" Art started.

"And that creepy caretaker man," Flinch said. "And we can find out more, can't we?" She sounded almost desperate.

"Of course we can," Meg told her. "Can't we, Art? The Invisible Detective's never been defeated before."

Art looked to Jonny for support. He at least should be able to see the sense in what Art was saying.

But Jonny wasn't there. He was across the warehouse, standing close to the door that led out to the loading area at the front. He had moved so fast that Art had not seen him go. Now he turned and ran back to rejoin them.

"There's someone coming," he said breathlessly. "I can hear them."

"Quick!" Art waved for them to hide.

Flinch was already gone, bundled impossibly inside a tight roll of carpet, only her eyes visible as they caught the light. Jonny ran across to hide behind a pile of underlay material. Meg ducked behind the carpet she and Art had been sitting on, and Art concealed himself further along from her.

For a while the warehouse was silent and still. Then the door where Jonny had listened swung open. Art peered around the edge of the pile of faded carpet. A figure stepped into the room and stood for a moment looking around. It was a man–tall, elderly and smartly dressed in a dark suit and top hat. He cleared his throat.

"Arthur?" he called. "I'm sorry. I mean, Art for short." He looked around with interest, and Art could see the man's face under the brim of the hat now as he angled his head back slightly. "I know you're in here, I just came to warn you . . ."

"Who is it?" Meg hissed at Art. "What's he talking about?"

Art waved for her to be quiet.

The man had cocked his head slightly, as if listening. Had he heard? "There's a watchman working his way along the street, checking the empty buildings." He threw his hands up, as if to show that it meant nothing to him if they wanted to stay hidden. "You have about ten minutes, probably. Just so you know," he added, and turned to go.

"Thank you, sir." Art stood up and called across the warehouse.

The man turned back, smiling now. "It's Charlie, remember?"

"Thank you, Charlie."

They looked at each other across the expanse of floor for a moment. Then Charlie said: "Look, I was just going for a cup of tea at the café at the station. I'd be honored if you would join me. And your friends, of course. Your throats must be dry with all this dust." He was watching as Jonny appeared from the shadows and Meg's head popped up above the carpet. "My treat, of course."

"Can I have cake?" Flinch's voice was edged with something close to awe as she uncurled from inside the roll of carpet. "Can I?"

Charlie laughed. "Of course you can, if you'd like."

Flinch beamed.

"Then we'd be delighted," Art said. "Thanks."

The night was thick and dark. Arthur Drake slept deeply, his dreams twisting through all the colors and hidden depths of the pebble clutched in his sleeping hand.

He dreamed about Cannon Street, about an old warehouse that used to store carpets, and about tea and cake at the station café. He dreamed about the Invisible Detective.

Just as the first light of the dawn nervously edged around the curtains of his room, he saw a man wiping at his moustache with a waxen finger and a large puppet's head turning slowly to watch him through glassy eyes. Then Arthur woke, the daylight chasing away his dreams and leaving only the suspicion of memories that were not his own.

CHAPTER 8

By the time they left the café, Jonny was late. He raced off at blurring speed and was soon lost to sight in the gathering evening. The others made their way back to the carpet warehouse.

Flinch waved to Art and Meg as she pushed the door closed, and Art and Meg turned back onto the street.

"I know you want to get back before your dad's home from work, and Flinch needs her sleep," Art said, "but we only have one lead really. Reggie Yarmouth and the Dog and Goose."

"What about Bessemer's exhibition?"

Art shrugged. "Coincidence, probably. Nothing really concrete anyway. Whereas we know that Yarmouth is missing."

"Ask at the Dog?"

"We don't have to drink anything," Art reassured her. "But we need to look a bit older than we are."

Meg considered this, biting at her lower lip and frowning. "What time?" she asked.

"Water?" Albert Norris was scandalized. "Water?" he repeated, his gruff voice full of disbelief. "This is a pub, you know!"

"I know," Meg said, her eyes as steely as her tone. "You do have some water?"

Norris shook his head, raised his eyes toward heaven and reached down a glass. "Water," he muttered, not quite under his breath.

"And a half pint of bitter," Meg said.

Norris blinked. "Right you are, miss," he said, at once deferential again. "Half of best bitter."

"Thanks," Art said to Meg.

Art sipped at the beer. It was cool on his lips and had a bitter aftertaste. He didn't like it and allowed some of the frothy liquid to trickle down the outside of the glass so it looked as though he'd been drinking.

They stood close to the bar, looking around for the best person to approach and hoping they did not look too conspicuous. Art was wearing the clothes he wore to school— gray flannel trousers and a white shirt—but with a large tweed jacket from his dad's wardrobe over the top. He'd had to roll the sleeves back in on themselves so they weren't too long. He hoped it wasn't too noticeable.

Meg was wearing one of her mother's dresses, which, she told Art, she had retrieved from the laundry basket. It was thin, pale blue cotton. She had a coat over the top, but had not done it up as it was far too big. Art was surprised and impressed at how grown-up she seemed. It looked as though she had smeared some lipstick on as well, but he didn't like to mention it. She would be either embarrassed that he had noticed or annoyed that he had to ask. He was not keen to discover which.

"You from around here, then?" A young man with a

blotchy red face was swaying at them, as if his feet had been fixed down while a gale blew. He was addressing Meg.

"Not too far away," Art said quickly, elbowing Meg gently to one side.

The man seemed disappointed. "Nice to meet you, then." He attempted to lurch away.

"We've got a friend who drinks here," Art went on, trying to keep the man's attention. "Recommended it to us."

"Oh, yeah?" He continued to move away.

"Perhaps you know him," Meg put in, smiling.

The man paused. "Maybe I do."

"Reggie," Art said. "Reggie Yarmouth." He made a point of looking around the pub. "He doesn't seem to be in tonight."

The man nodded, his eyes wandering as his head moved. "I know Reggie," he said. His voice was slurring now. "Ain't been in f'r'a while though." He leaned forward suddenly and Meg stepped back in surprise.

Art thought the man was about to faint. But instead he winked with an effort and tapped at the side of his nose several times with his index finger. The last time he missed and poked himself in the eye. "Disappeared, ain't he?" he said, rubbing at the injury.

"Disappeared?" Meg and Art exchanged interested looks.

"Not the only one neither."

"Oh?"

"My mate, Phil. He's gone and all." The man nodded again, violently. "It's true," he assured them. "Poor old Phil. Followed this girl out. Never saw him again."

Meg looked as if she was about to say something to this, but Art got in ahead of her. "What does your friend look like?"

"He's about my age, though he's got fair hair. His nose is bent where Mike Gunner taught him about cheating at cards." The man leaned forward again, staring at Meg through his bleary eyes. "Weren't you he was with, was it?" he demanded. "She was about your age, I reckon." He straightened up. "No," he decided. "No, weren't you." He turned away. "You don't walk funny."

"He meant Liza." Meg was firm.

"He *might* have meant Liza," Art said. "She isn't the only person who has a distinctive walk."

They were standing at the corner opposite Meg's house, waiting for the downstairs light to go out so Meg could slip back in.

"We should take another look at Bessemer's exhibition," she said. "Talk to Liza and see what she knows."

"All right," Art agreed. "The man who was with her did have fair hair. And his nose might have been crooked."

"Might have been?" Meg tilted her head to one side in the way she did when she knew he was lying.

"I can't be certain," Art told her. "I only caught a

glimpse as I knocked him flying. What if the light doesn't go out?"

"Then I'll take a chance that Dad's fallen asleep in the chair. Or he may not be back yet. Give it another few minutes."

Art nodded. "We could go tomorrow, after school. To the exhibition, I mean."

Meg was looking at the house. "I said I'd help Mum with some baking." Her voice was quiet. "I suppose I could . . ."

"Don't worry," Art said gently. "I'll go on my own. Or I might take Jonny."

Meg turned back to him. She ran her hand through her hair, as if unsure whether to speak. "You'd do better on your own," she said at last.

"Why? Jonny's no problem."

"I know." She sighed. "I just meant Liza's more likely to talk to you if you're on your own. That's all."

"You think so?" Art considered this. She might be right, Liza seemed to trust him.

Meg was still looking at him, her expression unreadable. Her face was in shadow as she stepped away from him. "I'm going in now." There was a trace of anxiety in her voice. "Wish me luck."

"Good luck," Art replied automatically. "You'll be all right?"

"I'll be fine."

Art watched her carefully open the door. She turned for a moment as she stepped inside and raised her hand in a desultory wave. Then she was gone and the door was closed once more.

Art waited for several minutes, listening for any sounds from inside the house. But he could hear nothing. As a distant clock started to chime the half hour, he made his way back toward his own home, already thinking of the exhibition, the strange puppets and Liza.

Old Creepy, as Flinch had called him, was taking money at the door. He bared blackened teeth at Art in what was perhaps meant to be a smile. Art was not sure if the old man recognized him or was this charming with all the customers.

"Tuppence each for kids," Creepy said in his cracked voice.

Art swallowed. He didn't have tuppence. "Liza said I could come back and have another look around," he said.

Creepy's eyes narrowed and receded into his wrinkled apple of a face. "Did she now?"

"For free." Art shuffled nervously. He could see the tall, thin figure of Bessemer approaching from inside the exhibition.

The old man nodded, wisps of hair waving around the fringes of his balding head with the movement. "Well now," he said slowly, teeth still on show, "if that's what Miss Liza said, then I'm sure it's all right, then." His eyes seemed to reappear as the "smile" dropped and he waved Art through. "You'd best be getting inside before the professor sees. I don't think he'd be so happy with letting people in for free."

Art took the advice, hurrying inside. Bessemer glanced at him with no sign of interest as he passed. Art heard Bessemer's reedy voice behind him.

"Ah, Crabtree. I need to talk to you about the park scene. Liza tells me there's a problem with the dog."

The park scene was about halfway around the exhibition. Art remembered how Flinch had been so taken with the little dog chasing the ball and the painted ducks on the backdrop. He hurried along, hoping Liza would be there.

He could immediately see the problem with the dog. There was a metal frame that supported the figure and presumably provided the means by which it bounced up and down after the boy's ball. Normally the frame would be hidden by the dog's own body, but the dog itself had become detached and was lying forlornly on its side. The boy's head was angled so that he seemed to be looking down sympathetically at the creature as he continued to dangle the ball out of reach. The dog's nose was twitching unconvincingly, its eyes were glassy and unfocused.

Liza was standing over the dog, looking as if she had been out for a stroll with the boy in the painted park when the dog collapsed. Art could see her lips moving, as if she was murmuring encouragement and sympathy to the animal. As Art drew closer, she looked up. Her large eyes seemed even wider than usual for a moment as she saw him. She stepped with difficulty around the boy and his prone dog, and moved to greet Art in her rolling, lurching manner. He tried not to look at the braces on her legs, tried not to see how the frame that should be holding the dog upright was made of the same dark metal.

"I'm glad you came," she said. "Thank you for helping me the other night."

Art grinned and shuffled his feet. "Well, you know . . ."

Liza started along the aisle and Art followed slowly beside her. "The professor went to get Mr. Crabtree," she said, glancing back at the toppled dog. "I expect he can fix him."

They paused at the pub scene. Art watched the puppet that recalled Reggie Yarmouth as it wiped imaginary froth from its moustache. In the cold glare of the lights it seemed even less likely that there was a connection between this exhibition and missing people.

"How long have you been helping Professor Bessemer?" Art asked.

Liza was staring at the scene, absorbed in the small movements, the detail of the figures, the artificiality of it all. "Forever," she said quietly. Then she turned toward him. "As long as I can remember, anyway."

Art looked away, embarrassed by the intensity of her gaze. "What about your parents? I mean, is he a relative or what?"

As Art spoke, he noticed a new figure standing at the

bar. Or at least, one he did not remember. It was a man of medium height with narrow shoulders.

"The professor is like a father to me," Liza was saying.

But Art was only half listening. There was something about the new figure that unsettled him. When he had first noticed it, before he looked at it properly, it had reminded him for a moment of the man outside the Dog and Goose. The man with Liza. Something about the silhouette, the shape, the stance, the way the figure held its head perhaps, even though it was wearing a crude mask.

But the hair was dark, the nose was straight and unbroken, and it was, after all, just a mannequin.

Liza was still staring intently at him. "I have to go," she said apologetically. "The professor wants me."

Art took his time looking around the rest of the exhibition. He was hoping that Liza would return, but she didn't. It was getting late and he ought to go home soon, he thought.

As he passed the steps that led up to where the queen was being crowned, he paused. The scene was toward the back of the old warehouse. The place looked so different, now that it was filled with these tableaux, but Art still knew the layout. Behind the flight of steps was a wall, and doors that led back to the offices and storerooms. One of them had been Flinch's bedroom and he wondered whether the bundle of old clothes and blankets that she had shaped into a sort of nest was still there. It would be easy to step over the rope that fenced off the path through the exhibits, slip around the back of the display. He could see if Flinch's bed was still there, maybe find some clues.

Flinch's room had been cleared out. Art wasn't really surprised. He stepped carefully inside and shut the door quietly behind him. Bessemer had turned it into a storeroom. Wooden chairs and a table were stacked in one corner, clothes, curtains, offcuts of material in another. Between them stood half a dozen or more of the life-sized puppets. Some of them were male, some female. Some were dressed and some were simply pale waxen figures draped in dustsheets. All of them had blank, unfinished faces staring off in different directions.

Carefully, almost delicately, Art lifted the sheet from one of the figures. It was taller than he was, the empty face staring sightlessly down at the floor. One arm was raised as if it was about to launch into a Shakespearean monologue; the other was folded across the chest.

Art tried to move the raised arm, pulling it down. But it was fixed firmly. He was not sure what the figure was made from. It was rigid, like Bakelite, yet soft to the touch, like wax. Except it was cold. He knocked on the figure's chest with his knuckles and it made a dull thudding noise as if the figure was hollow. Perhaps it was, perhaps Bessemer placed whatever mechanisms were required inside the chest to animate it.

Something on the wall caught Art's attention when he had finished his examination. It was a small display case, wooden with a glass front, fixed to the wall. Inside, Art could see what looked like a large stone or pebble. Apart from the stone, the case was empty. He peered through the glass, and as the light caught the stone he could see that it was a confusion of red and orange and blue. Was that a streak of silver running deep inside? It seemed almost to glow, as if lit from within by some hypnotic light. He felt his mind slipping into emptiness as he stared through the glass, and had to blink and shake his head to clear the strange feeling of numbness that crept over him for a moment.

It was as Art stepped away from the display case and turned to leave that he heard the voices.

They had been there, in the background, all along, but he had not noticed while he was preoccupied with the strange pebble. One voice, he could barely hear at all. The other was the thin, slightly nasal tone of Bessemer himself. The sound was coming from the next room, and Art tiptoed across to the wall and put his ear against it.

He could still make out very little, but occasionally Bessemer's voice was clear enough to make out a few words. ". . . find more subjects . . ." he said at one point. He mentioned "creating blanks," which Art took to refer to the mannequin figures before they were clothed and masked.

The other voice, the voice that Art could barely make out, spoke for a while. Probably Old Creepy, getting his instructions for the next day.

Then Bessemer was speaking again—more clearly now, as if louder and more insistent, or maybe just nearer to the wall. Art pressed his ear even closer, the cartilage painfully hard against the wood.

". . . latest addition is a prime candidate for the main event," Bessemer was saying. His voice died away for several seconds before Art could hear any more. "Height and weight are close enough, and the hair is obviously not a problem."

Art relaxed. A discussion of how to dress the latest puppet to grace the exhibition might be interesting, but it didn't help with the Invisible Detective's investigations, and Art would be late home if he didn't hurry. He was about to step away from the wall, about to slip out of the room and back to the main exhibition, when Bessemer's voice again carried to him.

"And the nose, of course, has been straightened and fixed."

Art froze. The second person was talking again now, and when Bessemer replied, his voice too was quiet and inaudible.

It's nothing, Art thought. Nothing at all. A puppet with a broken nose. Coincidence.

But there were so many coincidences. He opened the door as quietly as he could, holding his breath as he peered out into the corridor.

He glanced back into the room as he quietly closed the door behind him, but it was only later on his way home that he realized what he had seen. When he had first entered the room, all the figures were facing in different directions. The one he had tried to move had been looking down at the floor, others had been facing walls, or each other, or staring sightlessly into space.

As Art closed the door, as he glanced back, the figures were still fixed in position. Unmoving. Except that now each and every one of them had its blank waxen face turned toward the door, as if watching Art as he left the room.

"You're very quiet this morning," Arthur's dad said carefully as he attacked his cornflakes. "Everything all right at school?"

Arthur nodded. "Fine. No worries."

"That's good."

They finished breakfast in silence. Arthur could see his dad glancing at him from time to time when he thought Arthur wasn't watching.

"Dad," Arthur said, clearing away the breakfast things, "if I wanted to research our family tree or something, where would I start, do you think?"

"You can ask me." He considered. "Not that I can tell you much, I'm afraid. Gramps would be a better bet."

"On a good day, maybe," Arthur muttered, busying himself with the washing-up.

But his dad had heard, or at least caught the gist of it.

"His mind's still as sharp as ever. He's just a bit frail. Not surprising at his age." He wiped the table and tossed the cloth into the sink. It sent splatters of water over Arthur.

"Thanks, Dad."

"We should go over and see him this weekend. I've got Sunday off. You want to come?"

Arthur sighed. His dad never forced him to see Gramps, but there was always a guilt trip to live through when he didn't.

"Maybe," Arthur said, meaning *no.* He always felt awkward with his grandad.

"See how you feel."

"I might have homework."

"I thought this was your homework."

"Just interested," Arthur said. "That's all." There was never anything to talk about as they sat in his grandad's tiny room, or in the communal lounge with the television at full volume and old ladies asking each other what was happening now. And it smelled, not that he could ever mention *that.*

Dad was on his way out to get ready for work. "Well," he said, "if you don't want to talk to Gramps about it, why not try the library?"

"Maybe I will."

The door swung shut. As Arthur dried his bubbled hands on a tea towel, Dad's voice floated back to him: "At least the library doesn't smell."

CHAPTER 9

Flinch liked the new den, and the carpet she had shaped
into a bed was comfortable enough, but some nights, as she
lay awake listening to the rats scratching around looking for
food, she wondered how her own life was better than
theirs. She knew the answer—she had Art and Meg and
Jonny. They cared for her, she knew, and she loved them.

There were not many grown-ups that Flinch knew, and
even fewer she liked. Most of the people she saw on the
streets ignored her, looking away as if they hoped that, if
they didn't see her, she would somehow cease to exist. But
she had taken immediately to Charlie. She liked his manner and his appearance. She appreciated his kind words
and the fact that he did not look away, or make comments
about her appearance. She loved the cake he'd bought her.

So when Art led Charlie into the den that afternoon,
Flinch was delighted. She saw Meg and Jonny exchange
startled glances, but Flinch was not surprised. Of course,
Charlie was too old ever to be a Cannonier. But he was a
friend, and it was only natural that Art would let him come
to their den and their meetings now and again.

Charlie greeted them all politely, shaking hands—even
with Flinch. She giggled and held on to his hand. Charlie
smiled and led her to a roll of carpet where they sat
down together.

"I hope I'm not intruding," Charlie said as the others

found themselves perches nearby. Flinch could tell that he had seen Meg and Jonny looking at each other.

"Not at all," Art assured him. "I asked Charlie to join us," he explained to the others, "just for a few minutes." He paused, as if unsure what to say next. "I wanted to ask him a favor—on behalf of us all."

Meg and Jonny were paying close attention now. Flinch watched Charlie's face as she listened to Art speak. She could see the tiny dark dots on his chin where he shaved, the lines of his forehead where the skin was getting looser as he got older. She liked the way he had politely taken his hat off and she could see where it had flattened his lively gray hair in a circle about his head.

Art was speaking again. "Now, if anyone thinks this is a bad idea, then just say so and we'll forget it." Flinch could not imagine Art having a bad idea. "We have a small problem, which we've discussed before, and we need someone to meet my dad for a . . ." Art paused. "Discussion," he decided.

Meg's annoyed expression was slipping into realization. "You think Charlie . . . ?" Her voice faded.

Art nodded. "I think Charlie would make an ideal representative for Brandon Lake."

Jonny's mouth dropped open. "Would it work?"

"I don't see why not. If he's agreeable."

Charlie cleared his throat. "Agreeable to what, may I ask? I'm more than happy to help you all if I can, but I'm afraid this is going over my head. You want me to talk to your father about something, is that it?"

Flinch wasn't sure what Art meant either, so she was glad he had asked.

"Have you heard," Art asked, "of the Invisible Detective?" He was watching Charlie closely as he spoke.

"Only rumors," Charlie said. "He sits in a room somewhere around here and supposedly solves problems for people. Nobody ever sees him, not properly. Nobody really knows his identity." He frowned. "I don't know who he is, if that's what you're hoping, Art."

"We know who he is," Flinch said. She grinned at Charlie's confused expression.

"You do?"

Art cleared his throat, as if to warn the others to leave this to him. "We run errands for Mr. Lake," he said slowly. "Help him with his investigations, do you see?"

Charlie was looking around at them all, his mouth slightly open in surprise. "Let me get this straight," he said. "You are telling me that you—all of you—act as sort of Baker Street Irregulars for the Invisible Detective?"

"As what?" Flinch asked.

"Like the boys who helped Sherlock Holmes," Art told her. "In the stories."

"You don't believe us, do you?" Jonny said to Charlie.

"He believes us," Meg replied quietly.

"Yes. Yes, I do actually." Charlie stood up. He had his

hand over his mouth, head down in thought as he paced out a small circle. "It makes a lot of sense. After all, he does manage to stay 'invisible.' "

"The problem we have," Art said, while Charlie continued to pace slowly around, "is that the police want the Invisible Detective's help. They want to meet him. But Mr. Lake obviously doesn't want to attend this meeting himself. So he wants us to go."

"And you don't think they're expecting to meet a detective's representatives who are quite so young as you?"

"It's worse than that," Meg said. "The policeman who's meeting the Invisible Detective is Art's dad."

"He doesn't know we work for Brandon Lake," Art said. "It's secret, of course."

"Ah," Charlie said slowly. "Then I can see how that might present something of a problem." He smiled suddenly, and sat down next to Flinch again. "I think you had better tell me what the police want from this Invisible Detective." He looked around at them. "If I'm going to act as his representative."

Art was surprised and impressed by how well the meeting went. When Charlie had left, promising to contact Scotland Yard and arrange to see Art's dad as the representative of Brandon Lake, Art knew the others would tell him what they really thought of the idea. They did, but it was not what he expected.

"That was brilliant," Jonny said. "Just brilliant."

"Inspired," Meg told him. "It's a real stroke of luck that you met Charlie."

"I like him," Flinch said simply.

The next thing that Art expected to discuss was his suggestion that they sneak into Bessemer's exhibition after closing that night. He knew that Meg and Jonny would want to get home, and he was not keen to expose Flinch to unnecessary risk or danger. But he went over what he had discovered—or failed to discover—the previous evening. He listed his suspicions and described the coincidences and how they all seemed to relate back to Bessemer.

He considered telling them how he thought, but could not be sure, that the figures had turned toward him in the storeroom. But he decided that must be due to his imagination and nerves. He'd had strange dreams again last night—it was like he was sleeping in his own room but in a different bed. And the wallpaper was different, covered with large garish posters. Even the furniture seemed to have changed into white plastic wardrobes that were fixed onto the wall and reached right to the ceiling.

But he mentioned none of this. And that evening they watched the last visitors leave. Once again he helped Flinch up to the window and once again they watched and waited as she hauled herself inside and disappeared from view. After what seemed an age, the door creaked open and Flinch's grinning face appeared. Art held his finger to his lips for silence and they all slipped inside. Jonny pushed the door quietly closed behind them and bolted it again.

Meg and Jonny disappeared along the corridor toward the back rooms, leaving Art and Flinch to make their way through to the exhibition area. They were crossing the old machine room, making their cautious way through the debris and detritus of bygone days, when suddenly Flinch froze.

"What is it?" Art whispered.

"I heard something," she murmured. "Someone's coming."

Art could hear it too now—a door banging somewhere close by. Whoever it was might not be coming this way, but it was prudent to hide just in case.

In fact, they were just in time. No sooner had they ducked down into the shadows close to the wall than a figure emerged from the gloom ahead, picking its way across the room. It was stooped, moving slowly, and Art could hear him muttering curses under his breath. Creepy Crabtree was off on an errand he evidently was not enjoying.

As he drew level with them, halfway across the huge room, the old man paused, then stopped. His unpleasant little eyes caught the light as he turned toward where Art and Flinch were shying into the darkness. He stared across the room intently, almost malevolently, and Art was sure he had seen them. But then he grunted, rubbed at his leg where he might have caught it on a low bracket and continued his unenthusiastic progress.

When he was gone, Art and Flinch both exchanged relieved looks. Art blew out a long breath. "That had me worried," he confided. "Let's hope Meg and Jonny are keeping a good ear out."

"You think he'll catch them?" Flinch asked, her eyes wide with sudden worry.

Art smiled. "Meg can look after herself. And he'll never catch Jonny."

Most of the lights were off, but one area of the exhibition was still lit. Art and Flinch could see the glow of the light over the low partition walls that separated the different tableaux. The figures seemed even more eerie in the near-darkness. They were all switched off, but every so often Art or Flinch would turn suddenly as they thought one of the shadowy silhouettes had moved.

It was all imagination, of course. That was what Art whispered to Flinch as they edged closer to the light to see what was happening. That was what he wanted to believe. They peered carefully around the painted end of the park. The dog was back on its stand, staring forlornly up at the ball that hung just out of reach.

A spotlight shone down on the coronation. But the priest was still, crown poised over the queen's head. Neither of them moved. A third figure now stood silently beside them.

At the bottom of the steps Bessemer was talking quietly to Liza. Another of the life-sized puppets was propped up against a wall close by. The girl turned as Art peered out, as if she knew he was there. But a moment later she returned her attention to Professor Bessemer. Art strained to hear what they said. He could not make out Liza's soft words, but Bessemer's thin voice carried easily to where he and Flinch were hiding.

"That's as may be," he was saying. "But he still needs to manage the twenty-one steps."

Flinch was frowning up at Art, and he shrugged to show he had no idea what the man was talking about either. They turned back toward the coronation setting.

Bessemer was climbing the staircase. His tread was measured and steady, and Art counted off the steps as he went. Twenty-one. There were twenty-one steps to the top, where the queen waited patiently to be crowned. But Bessemer had turned to the other mannequin, the one leaning against the wall. He seemed to be talking quietly to it as he fumbled around behind it, perhaps adjusting some mechanism. Then the professor turned and walked carefully back down the stairs.

He nodded to Liza when he reached the bottom, and they both turned and looked back up. The figure at the top took a lurching step forward.

It seemed almost to topple down the first step, uncertain how to descend. Its movement reminded Art of how he felt when he misjudged the stairs at home and went down an extra step he didn't think was there. The figure paused, as if surprised at its accomplishment, and Art found himself marveling at the sophistication of the mechanism. Beside him, he was aware of Flinch watching with rapt interest.

Another falling step and again the figure paused. But now it was full in the spotlight and Art could see it clearly. It was the new figure from the pub scene—the one with the dark hair and straight nose. The figure he was so almost sure did not remind him of the man who had been with Liza outside the Dog and Goose.

Lurch, twist, almost-fall, and the figure had managed a third step. Far below, Bessemer was watching carefully, hands clasped together, almost as if he was praying that the figure would make it. And another step.

Art found he was counting under his breath. Somehow he felt sure that Bessemer and Liza were counting with him. Sixteen. He counted to sixteen before it happened.

On the seventeenth step, the figure fell. It seemed to misjudge the distance, though Art knew that the mechanism inside must treat each step exactly like any other. It continued to lean forward after its foot had found the step, its weight came slightly too far forward and it teetered for a moment. Bessemer took a step backward. Across the distance between them, Art heard Liza gasp in surprise and dismay.

The figure was toppling now, making no effort to save itself, oblivious of the danger. It came crashing down, face-first, sliding to the bottom of the staircase. Incongruously, its left leg was already trying to make the next step down as it came to rest at the base of the stairs. Then the whole body seemed to spasm, as if in shock, and it went still.

"Sixteen," Bessemer exclaimed. It was difficult to tell if he was impressed or disappointed. "So close, so very close." He slapped his right fist into his left palm. "A few more adjustments, a little more practice . . ."

Liza said something that Art did not catch, and Bessemer turned toward her.

"Yes," he replied. "Tonight. We'll try again as soon as I've made the adjustments."

Flinch was tugging at Art's arm and he looked down to see what she wanted. She nodded across toward the coronation tableau and it took Art a few moments to see what she was trying to show him. Then he caught his breath.

Meg and Jonny were standing beside the staircase, inching their way around. Any second they would look out from beside the stairs—straight at Bessemer. There was no way that he could avoid seeing them from where he was now, kneeling beside the fallen figure. Art waved his arm, trying to attract their attention, but neither Jonny nor Meg seemed to notice.

"They must have heard it fall," Flinch whispered. "Come to see."

Meg stepped out from cover. And immediately jumped back, pulling Jonny with her. Bessemer had, miraculously, chosen that same moment to stand up and shake his head. Somehow he managed to miss Meg and instead he turned his attention to the mannequin leaning against the wall.

Art could see that the figure had no mask, no features. Bessemer raised his hands and seemed to be fixing something to the figure's head. His hands moved, the stub of his middle finger jutting out at an angle. When he stepped away, Flinch caught her breath and Art just stared.

The puppet now had a face. It was not a crude mask with a wig and stuck-on moustache. This was a *real* face. The moustache, at least from where Art was standing, looked as if it had been carefully grown over a period of weeks or even months. The eyes stared back at Art, glassy and sightless.

Bessemer was shaking his head in answer to something Liza had said. "It knows," he said. "It knows what it has to do."

As Bessemer spoke, the puppet figure raised its hand, crooked its finger and wiped at the edges of its new moustache, as if to remove froth left by a pint of beer. Then it slowly turned and started hesitantly along the aisle between the exhibits. It walked slowly at first, as if getting used to the movement. But its confidence seemed to build quickly. The figure made its lurching, limping way toward the exhibition's exit.

Art and Flinch watched, openmouthed. Across the aisle, Meg and Jonny mirrored their expressions. Liza's face was set and impassive. Bessemer smiled with satisfaction as the figure hesitantly disappeared from view.

Seconds later, they all heard the sound of a door slamming closed. Then Bessemer's reedy voice carried across the silent exhibition.

"Good luck, Reggie," he said. But as he spoke, the satisfaction froze on his face. His eyes narrowed and he stared in anger across the aisle—straight at Art.

There were a few books on local history, but most of them were about London in general. There was nothing that seemed to deal in any detail with the Cannon Street area.

Arthur was prepared to be vague with the librarian. When the library was open late on Wednesday evening, it was nearly always the middle-aged woman with graying hair and her glasses on a chain around her neck. He didn't like the way she perched them on her nose to look at him. When he asked her advice, she always interrogated him about what precisely he was after. Arthur usually came away feeling drained and somehow guilty about the whole process of enquiring where to find information.

But local history was obviously not of interest to her. After some terse suggestions about books that Arthur was happy to tell her he had already found and looked at for himself, she waved him away toward the newspaper archives.

Microfilm was a new technology for him. Which was strange, as it was an old technology for the library. Today the newspapers would be stored on CD-ROMs and accessed on the computer. But nobody had the interest, the time or the money to transfer them. Arthur got the impression that for the sort of research that involved newspapers, people went to one of the bigger libraries or a specialist archive.

Once he had worked out which way the cartridge went into the reader and how slowly you had to turn the knobs to prevent the newsprint from rushing across the murky screen in a blur, Arthur found it fairly straightforward. There was a ring binder of typewritten subjects that purported to be an index, but it mentioned neither Bessemer's Paranormal Puppets nor the Invisible Detective. So Arthur started with the first date he recalled from the casebook, where he had read about them both, and worked his way through the papers from then on. The *Cannon Street Bugle* was a weekly publication, but being so close to Fleet Street seemed to have enthused its producers with the notion that they were but a step away from the Big Time, so each issue was crammed with news and opinion.

After an hour, the pages were shimmering in front of his eyes even when they weren't moving across the screen. He wasn't at all surprised that he missed the article entirely. He was on to the next paper when he found a reference back.

He almost missed that too. His attention was caught by an advertisement for a clock-maker and mender. *Edax Rerum*, it said in large, ink-hungry letters above a picture of a clock set at ten minutes to two. Italicized across the clock-face's smile was *Tempus Fugit.* Underneath the clock it said, *We have the time for you,* which Arthur thought was quite witty.

His eye caught the blurred shape of the words *Puppet Exhibition* as he moved on. He quickly turned the knob back again and eventually managed to line up the screen on the words:

> Last week our roving reviewer Miles Magassey
> visited a strange Puppet Exhibition in the area.
> This week he tries out some of the better tea
> shops. . . .

Last week. Arthur fumbled with the knob, turning back and back until he found the previous edition. And there it was:

> Miles Magassey's exploration of local culture
> this week takes him to Professor Bessemer's Ex-
> hibition of Paranormal Puppets.

CHAPTER 10

Immediately, Art ducked out of sight, dragging Flinch with him. But he knew he was already too late. He could hear Bessemer shouting, though the words were lost in the fury of his voice. The man's footsteps echoed around the exhibition as he strode toward where Art sat frozen on the floor.

Then he heard another voice. A nervous, high-pitched call from across the aisle.

"Oi—over here."

Somehow it gave Art the strength to move again and he allowed Flinch to help him quickly to his feet. He risked a quick look back around the partition. Jonny was waving at Bessemer, who was standing halfway across the aisle, looking from where Art was crouching to where Jonny was and back again, unsure which one of them to chase.

"Chase Jonny," Art murmured to himself. "Please chase Jonny." It wasn't a selfish thought. Meg could hide— Bessemer did not know she was there. If Bessemer came after Art and Flinch, he might catch them. But nobody could catch Jonny.

His mind made up, Bessemer turned and hurried across the aisle—toward Art. Behind him, Liza started her rolling, awkward walk and Art hoped she had not seen him, though he wasn't quite sure why.

"Come on," he said to Flinch, and together they ran.

It took Art and Flinch until they reached the back door to realize that Bessemer was not following. Had he simply given up the chase, Art wondered. There was no sign of Meg or Jonny either.

"Where are they?" Art gasped as they slammed the door shut behind them and gulped in the fresh evening air.

"They'll head back for the den," Flinch said. "We can meet them there."

"That's true," Art agreed. But he was worried that they weren't waiting at the back door. Had they been caught? Should he go back inside and try to find them, help them?

Art was still wondering what to do for the best as he and Flinch made their way along the alley to the front of the warehouse. A voice called out, startling him from his thoughts. He felt Flinch tense beside him, ready to run.

But it was Meg, calling from across the street, where she and Jonny were crouching in the shadows of a doorway.

Art looked around before he broke from the cover of the side passage to join them. The road seemed deserted; nobody at all was in sight. In fact, the only sign of life was Bessemer's large black car parked outside the main doors. The evening was drawing in and the air was murky with a mist of pollution and dust.

"You go first, Flinch," Art told her. He was still not convinced it was safe. An idea, an inkling, something, told him to be wary.

Flinch ran across the road, skipping up onto the pavement opposite as if she had not a care in the world. Art waited just a moment, then he followed.

He almost made it.

Art was staring right at the car when its lights suddenly came on. Dazzlingly bright, they were shining directly at him. For an instant, he froze. In that instant he realized what had unsettled him. The engine, he had heard, but not really taken in, the humming purr of the car's engine as it idled. Waiting for him.

The car was moving away from the curb. The engine throbbed noisily as the vehicle picked up speed, machine-gunning over the cobbles toward Art. A brief glimpse of Bessemer hunched at the steering wheel, then the windscreen was opaque as the car passed under a streetlight.

He was running again now. Shouting at the others that he'd see them later—Flinch knew where. He daren't even mention the den.

Running. Running for his life as the car swerved to follow him, tracking him as he desperately raced for the shelter of the houses opposite. He reached the other side of the road, leaping aside as the car mounted the curb and slammed across the pavement toward him like a hungry predator.

He heard the bottom of the car scrape on the ground, hoped it was damaged or at least delayed, ran without looking back. Art's feet stamped through a puddle, sending chill water splashing up his legs and into his shoes. He ran in the opposite direction from where he wanted to go, away from the other Cannoniers. The sound of the car's straining engine was loud in his ears, but whether it was real or imagined he did not know. He just kept running.

Down an alley—too narrow for a car to follow. He stumbled on as fast as he could. The image was imprinted on his memory: the car's headlight eyes burning at him, its radiator-grille mouth snapping at his face, its muscular wheels launching it toward him. A memory too deep and real and frightening for him simply to stop and catch his breath.

Only when he was at the other end of the alleyway, emerging gasping, shaking, into Queen Victoria Street, did he dare to stop. He had to be safe now, didn't he? But even as he dared to hope this was the case, a large black car charged through the gutter beside him, sending up a brown spray. Art jumped back, ready to sprint off again down the alley.

The car was a taxi, its sign illuminated as it hunted for customers. Art's gasps of relief and exhaustion tore at his chest, and he sank slowly down to sit on the pavement.

The figure in the shadows watched the boy from the other side of Queen Victoria Street. It followed him hesitantly, in a limping, rolling gait, as he walked slowly down toward Blackfriars station.

It was still with him as he looked around, seemed to satisfy himself that he had not been followed and turned back in the direction of Cannon Street.

When, eventually, he arrived at a disused warehouse that had once stored carpets and was now rotting with age and neglect, the silent figure stood awkwardly in an alcove further down the street. Still watching.

Art had made his way slowly back to Cannon Street. He'd checked over his shoulder frequently, caught his breath whenever a car went past. It was dark now and every car he saw looked black in silhouette.

Meg was waiting at the door of the den, bouncing on the balls of her feet with anxiety and impatience. "Thank goodness you're all right," she said, and for a moment Art thought she was going to hug him.

But instead, she pushed past onto the pavement. "I have to get home," she said. "Jonny's with Flinch."

"Thanks for waiting," Art called after her. Thanks for worrying about me, he thought.

Flinch was wide-eyed and close to tears. But relief wiped across her face when she saw Art.

Jonny laughed nervously. "Knew you'd be back soon," he said. "I was telling Flinch you'd be OK. Wasn't I, Flinch?"

Flinch did hug Art. "Jonny was worried," she said.

Art laughed. "So was I."

It was completely dark when Art finally got home. His dad had hinted he might be late back from the Yard, and Art half hoped he was still at work. He also half hoped that he was at home and would demand an explanation for Art's late arrival. Art had no idea what he would tell him, but to tell him *something* would be a relief.

The light was on in the living room. Art paused in the hall. Should he try to sneak past and get to his room, maybe pretend he'd gone to bed early and been in the house all the time? He wouldn't lie to his dad if asked, but he was less bothered about letting his father believe something that wasn't entirely true.

The question was answered for him. "Is that you, Art?" his father called out from the living room.

"Yes." He stepped tentatively into the room, aware of how he must look. His clothes were splattered with mud and still wet from the spray and the puddles. His hair was all over the place. He was red in the face from hurrying back from the den. His dad gave a short laugh and shook his head when he saw Art in the doorway. "You look how I feel," he said. "What happened to you?"

"I . . ." Should he tell him? "We were playing. It got late, I got lost." Art shrugged, trying to look calm about it. "I ran for miles. Puddles, cars—you know."

"I know." Dad stood up and came over to him. "It's very late," he said gently. "I was worried."

"Sorry. I'm fine, really."

"You sure?" Dad was looking at him as if he didn't quite believe this.

Now, Art thought, now is the time to tell him—tell him

everything, the Invisible Detective, everything. He opened his mouth, uncertain quite where to begin.

But Dad was turning away. "Hungry?" he asked. "I made sandwiches. Just cheese, but there's plenty."

"No," Art said quickly. "No, I'm not. Thanks. I just . . . well, it's been one of those days, you know, Dad."

"I know." He sounded like he did. "I had one of those too. All morning with Lord Fotherington. And tomorrow I have to go to the Institute of Aeronautical Technology, whatever that is."

"I'd better get some sleep." Art turned to go.

"Make sure you have a good wash first, won't you?"

Art sighed. "Yes, Dad." The stairs looked very steep. He gripped the handrail to pull himself up toward his bedroom.

"Oh, Art . . ." Dad was at the bottom of the stairs, looking up at him. "You know you were asking about Reggie Yarmouth?" Maybe Art looked confused. He felt cold and numb. "The man from the Dog and Goose everyone thought was missing."

"Thought?" His voice was barely a croak. His throat was dry and the blood was thumping in his head.

"Yes. Extraordinary thing. Seems he's turned up again. Had a fall or something. I'll know for sure tomorrow. I've got some new duties for a while, and I'll have to see him about that."

"What happened to him?" Art hardly realized he was asking the question.

"Visiting his mother, apparently," Dad said. "Fell down the stairs."

In his mind's eye, Art remembered the lumbering figure that had shuffled out of the exhibition earlier that evening. It seemed like days ago.

"Fell down the stairs?"

He remembered how it had struggled to drag one foot after the other on its way from the coronation exhibit to the main entrance.

"Yes." Art's dad smiled sympathetically up at him. "I gather it's left him with quite a bad limp."

In the event, the article told Arthur very little about Bessemer's exhibition. After a brief description of the attraction and some comments about how impressive it was, the whole thing went downhill. He quickly lost interest.

Arthur reckoned he had a better idea of what the exhibition had been like from the Invisible Detective's casebook. That at least had a floor plan sketched and labeled, as well as Art's scribbled accounts of his various visits.

Most of Miles Magassey's attention was taken up with wondering what mechanism Bessemer used to animate his puppets. Magassey favored clockwork, and spent some time showing off how much he knew about eighteenth- and nineteenth-century automata—including a chess-playing Turk which was apparently the marvel of the age and which nobody had yet managed to figure out almost 150 years later.

Arthur wondered idly if the mystery of the chess player had been solved now that another seventy years had passed. He was disappointed not to find more, and it was already closing time and they were turning out the lights. Dad was working late tonight, so there was no rush to get home. Perhaps he would pick up fish and chips on the way.

A car skidded to an abrupt halt beside him as Arthur crossed the road outside the library. It was an access road, leading to a small parking lot at the back of the building, and he had not bothered to look. No one ever used the road.

It was the librarian. She was winding down her window. She was wearing her glasses and Arthur noticed with amusement that they matched the headlights of her car.

"Sorry," he mumbled, expecting her to rail at him about looking where he was going.

She glared over the top of the glasses. "Did you find what you were looking for?" she demanded.

That surprised him. "Oh, um," he said. "Yes and no. Sort of." He shrugged.

The car pulled away again, as if she had no interest in the answer, just in asking the question. "You could always try the Internet," she shouted at him as she pulled out onto the main road without looking.

CHAPTER 11

Skulking in a narrow passageway between Stoney Street and Winchester Walk was not Peter Drake's preferred way of meeting with the public. But Daft Derek had not come by his name accidentally and he seemed convinced that anywhere less secluded—and possibly less smelly—might mean they were seen and overheard.

There were the remains of a rotting cabbage lying in the narrow gutter, and the buildings either side of the alley seemed to shake whenever a train crossed the bridge to Cannon Street station on the other side of the Thames.

"Two men," Derek said, holding up three fingers. "Two of them, that's the word on the street."

"You're sure?" Drake asked.

Derek looked confused. "One of them's certainly a man," he said.

"No, I meant—"

But Derek wasn't listening. He was looking around furtively to make sure there was nobody else within earshot. Drake was half expecting him to edge the cabbage along with his boot to check underneath.

"One of 'em's tall and thin," Derek whispered. His whisper was louder than his normal speaking voice and laced with spittle. Fortunately the man smelled so much that Drake was already keeping his distance. Derek's clothes were stained and torn, a piece of frayed string holding his trousers tight at the waist. He had several days of stubble on his chin—dark and greasy like his hair, but showing some gray. His eyes were tiny glints in his grimy, discolored face.

"You've seen him?" Drake asked.

"Might have." That meant yes, but somehow Derek could never bring himself to say the word outright. "He's missing the top of his finger. Look." Derek held up his own middle finger, bending it back at the knuckle to demonstrate.

Drake was not sure about this. There might be something in what Derek said. There again, he might have invented the whole story, or picked up some thirdhand gossip that was nothing to do with missing people at all. "What about the other man?" he asked.

Drake shrugged. His clothes rippled with the movement and bits of dried mud fell off. "Nobody's seen him. Not proper. Shorter, sort of crouched, apparently. Moves like an old man, some say."

"And they've been seen actually abducting people in the vicinity of Cannon Street?"

"The what?"

"*Near* Cannon Street."

"Oh, yeah." Derek nodded. "Well, no. Not as such."

Drake sighed. "Then what, as such?"

He shrugged again. "Just sort of hanging around, like. But on days when people have gone missing. They watch, you know. Waiting," he added ominously.

Drake nodded back. "Thank you," he said. "That's very . . . helpful, Derek."

Daft Derek leaped away from Drake, cowering in the shadows. "Shh!" he hissed. "Don't say my name. Someone might be listening."

Drake sighed and fumbled in his pocket for some loose change. "It's too much to hope, I suppose, that you'll spend this on a decent meal? Or some soap?" He dropped the coins into Derek's waiting hand.

"Gawd bless you, sir." He counted the coins carefully, tongue licking out of the corner of his mouth. "Sorry about that business with me name. But, you know. Best to be careful."

"I'll be careful," Drake assured him. "In any case," he added as he turned away, "we were probably photographed coming down here anyway." He grinned to himself as he imagined Derek's expression behind him.

There was a muffled clinking as Derek stuffed the coins into a pocket. "Don't say that, sir," he hissed as Drake continued down the alleyway, toward the sunlight at the other end. "If they knew I was talking to you . . ." His voice tailed off.

"They'd think I was out of my mind," Drake muttered. "Whoever they are."

Moments later, Peter Drake checked his watch, blinking in the harsh sunlight and glad to be able to breathe air that was tinged only with the usual smells of London. He had a little time. Time enough to walk the route, he decided.

He crossed over London Bridge and walked along Cannon Street. The sun dipped behind clouds as he passed St. Paul's and kept going into Ludgate Hill. He turned up the collar of his coat. Ludgate Hill became Fleet Street, and before too long the sun came out again and he was on the Strand. Sergeant Drake paused outside a large building in Aldwych. This was the end of the route, now he would walk back along it, tracing it to its source—the Institute of Aeronautical Technology in Russell Square.

He timed the walk, though of course they would use a car the following day. It took him a little under twenty minutes at a brisk pace. Then he was standing in front of the imposing Regency building that housed the institute.

Inside, a man in an air force uniform sat at a desk, checking names against a list as people came in. "Can I help you, sir?" he asked curtly as Drake came through the doors and looked around the large foyer. The floor was tiled in marble and a flight of stone steps rose majestically behind the man.

Drake showed his badge. "Sergeant Drake, assigned to Royal Protection."

The air force man nodded deferentially. "The dinner tomorrow, of course, sir. I'm to send you up to the Sopwith Room, sir."

The Sopwith Room was off a corridor about halfway

up the stairs. It was paneled in dark wood and dominated by a large matching table. Drake seated himself at one end of the table.

Almost immediately, a door opened in the paneling—a door Drake had not even realized was there—and a man stepped into the room. He was tall and in a dark blue uniform, complete with peaked cap. A handlebar moustache hid most of his mouth, but his blue eyes twinkled with amusement.

"Sergeant Drake?" His voice was clipped and efficient. "I'm Captain Smithers." He whipped off his cap to reveal perfectly combed black hair beneath and marched over to where Drake was sitting. Smithers extended his hand as Drake stood up. "Freddie Smithers, actually."

They shook hands, then both sat down at the table.

"I'm acting as liaison for the Duke of York's visit tomorrow, the dinner and speech and everything," Smithers explained. "That means I liaise with you Royal Protection people as well, apparently. All new to me, though, I'm afraid. So you may have to talk me through it."

"I have to confess I'm new to it too," Drake told him. "Though I'm sure his lordship will be in safe hands while he's here. But I thought I'd better have a quick word with the people he'll be in direct contact with, check they're happy."

"By all means. Seems sensible."

"And I'd like to see the room where he'll be."

Smithers nodded. "The duke will prepare for his speech

in here, and retire here afterward before he goes on to the memorial ceremony in Aldwych. I can show you the banqueting hall whenever you like. That's pretty much it."

"And the staff?"

"Some civilians. But they know the protocol. Bit of a crisis when the institute's valet went AWOL for a while. Absent without leave," Smithers explained, in case Drake did not understand.

Drake nodded. "Yes, I can imagine. Can't have the king's brother coming around for dinner and no valet. Let's start with him, then, if he's available."

"Righto." Smithers stood up. "I'll send him in. The valet is basically responsible for ensuring the Duke of York has everything he needs. He'll help his lordship prepare in here, and be on hand afterward in case he needs anything else. Pretty straightforward."

Smithers opened the door in the paneling and leaned out into the room beyond. Drake could hear his clear tones as he called, "Ready for you now, Reggie."

A few moments later, Smithers stepped aside and Reggie Yarmouth limped into the room.

It took Drake the rest of the morning and the early part of the afternoon to interview the various staff. After that he spent some time with Smithers looking around the banqueting hall. Smithers explained where the tables would be, and together they went through the guest list. Mostly it was Royal Air Force personnel, with some "boffins," as

Smithers described them, together with wives and a sprin-kling of Cabinet ministers.

"I hope they like the food," Drake said with a laugh.

Smithers smiled. "I gather there's more concern about the wine, actually, sir."

It was almost two o'clock when Drake left the banqueting hall. Plenty of time to get to his meeting with the so-called Invisible Detective at Cannon Street station. He was not sure what to expect from the meeting, but he doubted it would be of much more use than his conversation with Daft Derek.

As he made his way down the stairs to the foyer, Drake realized he was counting the steps. Fifteen, sixteen, seven-teen . . . How many steps there were from the ground floor to the banqueting hall was the sort of useless information that Gilbertson might just expect him to have at his finger-tips. Nineteen, twenty, twenty-one.

He smiled and nodded at the air force man on the desk at the door. Twenty-one. If Gilbertson wanted to know, there were twenty-one steps in all.

There was a light drizzle in the air as he walked back toward Cannon Street. If it got any heavier, Drake thought, he might take a cab. But he was in good time and the clouds seemed to be thinning. The sun struggled through as he approached the station with ten minutes to spare.

The café was busy with people waiting for trains. Drake

found himself a table in the corner, from where he could see the door, and ordered a cup of tea. He had not had lunch, he realized. Maybe, after his meeting with the Invisible Detective, he would hang on for a toasted tea cake.

The tea was very hot. Drake cupped his hands around it as he thought through his visit to the institute. Reggie Yarmouth had been quiet and polite, as you would expect from a good valet. He had seemed embarrassed by Drake's enquiry about his leg and how he was after his fall, wiping at his top lip in a nervous manner. But he certainly seemed to understand his duties for the next day.

"Sergeant Drake." The voice was quiet and composed. Drake looked up in surprise. "How nice to see you again so soon."

Drake swallowed. "I thought you were at the Yard today, sir."

Lord Fotherington smiled. "May I?" He indicated the chair opposite Drake.

"Er, well, I am expecting someone."

Fotherington nodded. "This won't take long," he said. He turned and waved to the waitress, who was delivering a pot of tea to a nearby table. "Tea, please. When you have a moment."

"Really, sir," Drake said hesitantly, "if you need some more information, shouldn't we discuss it at the Yard?" He glanced at his watch. It was exactly three o'clock. He looked over to the door. A man was just leaving, a young man with straggly hair. A few tables away a grubby-looking youth with dark hair hidden beneath a flat cap turned away. Drake caught sight of his profile and there was something familiar about it. The youth seemed to be trying to catch the eye of a young woman with curled red hair on the other side of the café.

"I'm not after information, Drake," Lord Fotherington was saying. "You were most forthcoming and helpful in our discussions yesterday, thank you." He leaned aside to allow the waitress to put his tea down in front of him.

Drake was hardly listening. What if the Invisible Detective arrived now and saw he was not alone? He looked back at Fotherington and realized that the elderly man was staring back at him intently with his pale eyes. His mass of white hair seemed to shimmer in the artificial light. "Well, as I said, sir . . ." His voice tailed off. The dark-haired youth was watching him over the top of his teacup as he drank.

"You are waiting for someone." Fotherington nodded. "I know. In fact, I know who you're waiting for."

"What?" Drake frowned. He had a strange feeling in the bottom of his stomach.

Across the table, Lord Fotherington, special representative of the home secretary, sipped his tea and nodded in satisfaction. "That's very good," he murmured. "Yes," he said to Drake. "You may find this hard to believe, in fact I find it quite difficult myself. But *I* am the man you're waiting for. I represent the Invisible Detective."

There was nothing of interest on the London websites that Arthur looked at on the computer at home. Most of them listed events and exhibitions that had happened and were over. None of them were at all interested in local history.

The search engines he tried were no more help. Whatever he searched on returned either nothing at all or hundreds of links to things that seemed not at all related to what he'd typed in.

The school Computer Club met on Thursdays. "Club" was a bit grand. All it meant was that Squirrel stayed behind to grade papers and allowed anyone who wanted to come and use the computers till five-thirty, when he went home. His real name was Mr. Wirrel. But what hair he had left was gray tufts and his cheeks looked as if he were saving bits of his lunch for later, so the kids called him Squirrel.

Squirrel knew almost nothing about computers. If you had a question, he would nod and smile and ask all the other boys if any of them could help. It was usually only boys who stayed for the club—and usually it was just Kenny and Dibbs. They didn't need any help with the computers. They lived on computers. They tolerated Arthur, as he had some notion of how to surf and once got the high score in Stagnation.

But this week the new student teacher, Mr. Hanshaw, had

made it known he would be staying for Computer Club and was happy to give beginners' training to anyone who wasn't sure how to get started. Arthur didn't reckon that Mr. Hanshaw was an especially good teacher. But he was pleasant enough and it didn't surprise Arthur that several of the older girls had decided to stay behind and avail themselves of his offer of help.

Arthur managed to get the computer in the corner furthest away from the chattering girls. He tried to blot out the sighs of exasperation and annoyance from Kenny. Dibbs just giggled uncontrollably, which was even more distracting. By half past five, when Squirrel got up to leave, Arthur had had enough. Mr. Hanshaw was happy to stay for a while, and Kenny and Dibbs were happy to keep using the school's machines rather than go home to theirs. But Arthur decided he might as well pack it in. He'd tried a few more websites without success, and browsed every conceivably relevant subject on two of the encyclopedia disks the school had. There was a third, but the box was empty and Arthur couldn't be bothered to go hunting for it.

"Good ses?" Mr. Hanshaw asked, looking up from Sarah Bustle's browser as Arthur went past. Why did he have to talk like that?

"OK," Arthur admitted. He paused, it was worth asking—nothing to lose. "Mr. Hanshaw, do you know of any websites with local history on them?"

Mr. Hanshaw thought about this. "You mean local as in around here?"

"Well, yes." Sarah Bustle was glaring at Arthur. He ignored her.

"No, I don't think I do. Was it just general interest?"

"Sort of. Thanks." He turned to go.

"Sorry. If you've got a specific question, though," Mr. Hanshaw said as he returned his attentions to Sarah Bustle, "you could always ask the Invisible Detective."

CHAPTER 12

A sudden shaft of sunlight lit the front of the old warehouse as Art approached it. The light seemed to angle down from the cloudy sky and picked out a short figure standing outside. Liza.

She was watching Art as he made his way slowly along the pavement. He did not want to get too close, did not want to risk being seen by Bessemer or Crabtree—he was sure it was them in the car the previous night, chasing him. Trying to kill him. But he did want to see Liza. She might need his help. He did not like to abandon her to whatever fate might have in store.

Art's dilemma was solved when Liza turned slightly to look back into the exhibition doorway, then started to walk toward him. She was hurrying as much as the braces on her legs would allow, rolling from side to side as she gained speed. Her expression was set as she approached and Art could only begin to imagine the pain she must feel as she shambled awkwardly along.

He walked slowly, furtively, toward her, keeping his eye on the exhibition entrance and remaining ready to run if Bessemer or Crabtree should appear.

Liza had almost reached him when she fell. Her foot turned on an uneven edge of the pavement and slipped from under her. Art saw it happen, as if in slow motion. Somehow he knew even before it happened that she was about to fall.

He ran forward as she staggered, trying to regain her balance. Her arms flailed and her other leg buckled.

"Liza!" His shout was instinctive as he leaped forward, arms outstretched. He caught her, just. She fell toward him, her hands out to break her fall, and he grabbed her under the arms. She was a dead weight, unable to angle her legs to support herself, and Art stood motionless for a while, holding her. He was surprised how heavy she was against him. He could feel his heart beating against her body. Their faces were side by side. They each held their breath.

Somehow she managed to pull herself upright again. He did not let go until he was sure that she was standing firm, then she pushed him gently away. Art coughed, embarrassed.

"Are you all right?"

"Thank you," she said. Her voice was as calm and melodic as ever.

"My pleasure. It could have been a nasty fall."

"I'm used to falling," she said. She was staring at him with her large eyes. "You were at the exhibition last night. I saw you."

Art nodded. "So did the professor. He came after me in his car. I was lucky to escape."

"I know."

"Liza?" He put his hand gently on her arm. "What's going on here? What's Bessemer up to, him and Crabtree?"

"I . . ." She hesitated. "I don't know," she said at last. "But it's not good."

"Is it to do with the missing people?"

She did not answer.

"I want to help," Art told her. "I want to help *you*."

She nodded, her expression fixed as she considered this. She swung around and looked back down the road. "I have to get away," she said slowly. "I have to get away from *him*. From his influence." She turned back toward Art and fixed her gaze on him again. "You have the will," she was saying. "The strength of mind to do it."

"Do what? Anything—tell me." He could feel how desperate she was.

"To help me escape, get away."

"There is somewhere you can hide. For a while anyway." He was thinking of the den. Thinking of how she could stay there with Flinch for a time. Trying not to think of what Meg might say to the idea.

"Tomorrow," she said. "Meet me tomorrow night at the exhibition."

"Why not come now?"

"I would not get far before the professor missed me. I cannot walk fast," she said, looking down at her legs imprisoned in the metal cages that held them rigid. "He would soon find me. And he can make me come back. He can make me do anything. But tomorrow night, we shall have more time. And there are some things I need to prepare. Tomorrow. At ten o'clock."

"Of course."

She tilted her head slightly as she looked at him, her

hair falling to the side in a mass. "Did you find the store-room, next to the professor's office?" she asked.

He nodded. "With the puppets or whatever they are."

"And the lodestone." Her voice was slightly husky. "In the glass case on the wall. Did you see that?"

"Yes." He could remember it so clearly—the translucent pebble with its depths of color and light. For a moment he felt himself again falling into the image. "I remember."

"It is mine," she said quietly. "I must have it back. To-morrow, when you come for me, you must get the stone. I shan't be free unless you have it."

Art frowned, wondering why she could not get it her-self if it was hers. Perhaps the display case was too difficult for her to open. "All right."

She held out her hands and he took them in his. They were cool and smooth. The fingers were long and slender, with perfect nails. Everything about her was perfect, except her crippled legs. But somehow they enhanced her beauty. "Tomorrow night," she said.

"Ten o'clock."

All too soon, she pulled gently away, turned ponder-ously and made her uneven way back toward the exhibition.

The mist was rolling in like smoke by the time Art arrived at the den. The buildings on the other side of the street were shadows; people on the pavement were blank silhouettes.

"Is Charlie coming?" Flinch asked as soon as Art was inside.

"Later," he said. "He was meeting Dad this afternoon. He was going to tell him about the Paranormal Puppets."

Flinch nodded seriously and flopped down on a roll of carpet. The dust sprayed up like the mist outside. Meg and Jonny were not there yet. Jonny was coming after he'd been home for tea. Meg would turn up when she could—it depended on whether her father was home yet.

Art had been home and collected bread and cheese from the parlor. He spread his handkerchief out on a less dusty bit of floor and displayed the meager picnic. "You hungry?"

Flinch was always hungry by the end of the day. She leaped down from her perch and sat cross-legged beside Art, stuffing bread into her mouth. He was amazed she could get so much in at once without making crumbs. He was surprised she could eat it so quickly so dry. There was a leaking pipe at the back of the warehouse where they collected the drops of water in a tin cup. He went to get it and Flinch paused to gulp down the cold liquid before starting on the cheese.

"After last night," Art said, "I think the Invisible Detective will have some more information to pass on."

"The chase." Flinch's eyes were wide with the remembered excitement. She was gnawing her way around a lump of cheese, scraping off slivers with her front teeth.

"And that business with the Reggie Yarmouth puppet. I wanted to tell Dad last night . . ." He shrugged and looked away, thinking of Liza. "Better if it comes from the Invisible Detective, though," he said. "Dad's more likely to believe him. I hope."

Jonny joined them at just after six. "It's getting thick out there," he said. "You can hardly see to put one foot in front of the other."

By the time Meg arrived, they could see the fog close against the broken discolored windows high above them. The air in the warehouse was damp and clammy as the mist crept in to join them. A door banged in the distance, at the back of the building.

"That'll be Charlie," Art announced with confidence.

But he was wrong.

There were three of them. The priest, the barman and the boy from the park. For several moments, the Cannoniers just stared at the incongruous sight.

The priest led the way, lurching toward them from the back of the huge storage area. His hands moved in unison, up and down, just as they had while crowning the queen at the exhibition. But they were not holding a cardboard crown. Instead, each hand held a small ax that chopped again and again as the bizarre figure approached them.

The barman was twisting his hand, as if he thought he was still holding the tea towel he used at Bessemer's pub to dry the beer glass. But what twisted viciously in front of him now was a knife. There was a mist of condensation on the metal blade.

The boy still held his hand out for the dog. But the dog was gone and in place of a ball on a string there was a metal spike. All three of the figures stared glassily ahead as they stumbled across the wooden floor, their feet beating out a steady heartbeat of sound.

The four children stared in horror and disbelief. Art recovered first, taking a step backward as he caught sight of the dull light reflecting off the spike of metal in the boy's inhuman hand.

"Run!" he shouted. "Get out on the street, where there are people."

Jonny was already on his way—flying past the priest, who moved too slowly to intercept him. An ax crashed through the air where Jonny had been a half second earlier. Once clear, he turned to see how the others were doing. His face was an anguished mask of indecision—run or stay and help?

"Go!" Art screamed at him. "Find Charlie—or anyone."

With an expression of relief and anguish, Jonny turned and sped away.

Three on three now. The priest had turned his attentions to Meg, who was cowering back. She stepped away from him, caught her foot in a pile of carpet fragments and went flying—just as an ax cut through the air above her.

Immediately Art was there, pulling the girl to her feet even as he sidestepped the barman's blade. As he pushed Meg clear, Art grabbed a handful of carpet and pulled at it.

The material was flaking in his grip like old paper. It tore free and he swung it around in time to intercept the knife.

The barman seemed not to notice. The knife continued to twist. But now a wad of material was covering the blade. Showers of dust and frayed wool fell away as the lurching nightmare took another faltering step toward Art.

Flinch seemed the least affected of them all. She waited for the boy to get close. Her face was set and her eyes never left the spike that he thrust out as he came. As soon as he was within range, Flinch lashed out with her foot, kicking the boy hard between the legs.

The small figure rocked back, staggering. Then it seemed to right itself and stepped forward again. Flinch kicked out again at the metal spike, sending it spinning away to clatter to the floor several yards away.

"Follow Jonny," Art screamed at her.

Unworried now by the boy's ineffectual hand movements, Flinch edged around him and ran.

Meg and Art were cornered. The life-sized puppets of the priest and the barman had herded them across the warehouse toward the wall. A flight of broken wooden steps rose to a gantry, but otherwise there was no escape. Art was making for the steps when he shouted to Flinch to go. But once she was gone, the boy moved to cut him off.

They looked from one of the puppets to another. The incessant movement of the barman's knife had dislodged the carpet and the blade was free once more. The priest's axes rose and fell with a steady, deadly rhythm. Neither Art nor Meg said anything as they continued to back away, toward where the boy waited for them at the bottom of the stairs.

When they were almost there, they both turned. Instinctively, Art and Meg knew what to do. Art grabbed for the boy's jabbing hand, while Meg grabbed his other arm. Whatever it was made from, the puppet was hard, unforgiving—and heavy. They staggered under the weight as Art struggled to lift it, turn it and, with Meg's help, propel the automaton toward its fellows.

The boy skidded unbalanced across the floor. He staggered, trying to retain his balance, and crashed into the priest. An ax bit down into the boy's neck and his head twisted under the impact. Then he fell, legs still working. The priest stepped forward, oblivious of the figure at its feet. A moment later he caught his legs in the struggling boy and toppled slowly over.

There was just the barman now. But they were at the stairs.

"I bet he can't climb—remember the trouble they had last night," Art gasped.

Meg was already running up the stairs. But she did not get far. Art turned to follow, in time to see Meg take the fourth step. In time to hear the crack as the wood gave way beneath her weight. She fell forward with a cry and suddenly the whole staircase was collapsing. A mass of rotten timber smashed down. The sound was incredible, echoing around the warehouse—the sound of Meg's scream as she fell.

Art was able to leap clear. But Meg was lying in the shattered wooden debris, gasping in pain. And the barman was stepping slowly but surely toward her.

As soon as Arthur was home, he went straight to the computer.

"In one of your sociable moods, I see," Dad called to him as he passed the lounge.

"Busy, Dad. Homework and stuff." He was up the stairs already. "I'll be on the computer."

"I want to use the phone later, so don't stay on it too long," Dad called back.

The computer was in the tiny room upstairs that was supposed to be the spare bedroom. If you took out the small desk with the computer on it, there might be enough space for a single bed. Just.

It took an age to boot up. Arthur was drumming out a frustrated rhythm on the desk in front of the keyboard as he waited. Once the computer was running, it took forever to connect over the phone. Eventually, he was able to start the browser and type in a web address: invisible-detective.com.

Why did everything about computers take so long? You kept hearing how much quicker they were getting, yet everything was still so slow. The banner at the top of the page appeared first. Then gradually, graphic by graphic, other elements popped up. Arthur watched in amazement.

The Invisible Detective, the page declared.

> Ask your questions of the Invisible Detective
> who lives in the Internet and await the answer.
> It's as simple as that.

There were a couple of entry boxes where you could type and a "Go" button. Lower down the page were some sample questions to show you what you could ask. They varied from, "How do I make a Spanish omelette?" to "Who won the Battle of Marston Moor?" Other examples included, "Where's the best place to buy electrical goods in Princeton?" and "How long is a piece of string?"

Arthur read through the instructions twice. You typed in your question and your e-mail address and then hit "Go." You could ask anything you liked, and the answer, or in rare cases an apology for not finding one, would be e-mailed to you. There were the usual notes about privacy and copyright, and a warning that difficult questions might take the powerful search engines and software a little while, so wait a week before asking again.

There was also a line of buttons which included "About Us," "Legal Statements" and "Background—the *Real* Invisible Detective."

CHAPTER 13

Meg tried to pull herself up, finding the barman's knife angled close to her face. The knife thrust forward and she managed to jerk her head away just in time.

But the next blow would connect. Even as Art launched himself across the space between them, he knew he would be too late. He might manage to deflect the heavy figure, but the knife would already be thrust.

Meg's eyes were wide in horrified surprise. Art was in midair. The knife was moving.

Then came the shot. An echoing percussion of sound that rang explosively around the building. Suddenly the knife was gone and the automaton's wrist was a stump of splintered wood jabbing at Meg.

Art's shoulder knocked into the heavy figure, sending it sprawling away from Meg. Art was on his feet again at once, turning back to help her. But someone else was already pulling Meg gently to her feet with one strong hand. The other hand was holding the service revolver that had shot away the knife.

The barman remained on his feet. He was facing the wooden wall, still walking, but only succeeding in pressing himself against the wood with every heavy step.

"Are you all right?" Art asked Meg.

"I am now," she said through tears of pain and relief.

"Then let's get out of here."

"An excellent idea," Charlie said. "Jonny and Flinch are waiting outside."

The fog was so thick now that you could cut it with a knife. Charlie led Art and Meg along the side of the warehouse to where Jonny and Flinch stood waiting. Jonny looked drawn and afraid. Flinch was shivering with the damp, and Charlie took off his coat and draped it over her shoulders. The coat almost drowned her, but the girl pulled it tight.

Somewhere in the distance, muffled by the fog, Art could hear a car pulling away. "Guess who?" he murmured.

"This way," Charlie said. "It's not far. If we walk briskly."

"Where are we going?" Meg asked. She seemed to be walking more easily now, but she was obviously in pain from her fall.

Before the old man could answer, a dark shadow loomed out of the fog ahead of them, tall and sinister. It slowly solidified into the reassuring shape of a policeman.

"Constable," Charlie said at once, "I need you to do something for me."

"Excuse me, sir," the constable retorted, "but I've been told there was some shooting over this way."

"There was," Charlie told him. He pulled his wallet from his jacket pocket and took out a card.

The policeman stared at it, his mouth open. "I see, sir," he said quietly. "How can I help?"

"Do you know Detective Sergeant Drake? Peter Drake?"

The constable nodded.

"Then please find him. Immediately. Give him my card and ask him to join us at my house as soon as he can."

"Sir." The policeman turned quickly, his cape swirling in a haze of mist. He was at once swallowed by the fog.

"What will you tell him?" Meg wanted to know.

"What happened this evening. Everything you have discovered about this strange exhibition. But," he went on, "I think we'll keep the details of the Invisible Detective's role in this to ourselves, shall we?"

"Oh, yes!" Flinch exclaimed at once.

"You were just exploring possibilities on your own. Agreed?" He smiled kindly at Jonny, who was nodding nervously. "No need for the detective to get involved, unless of course he wants to."

It was difficult to tell where they were going in the fog. The evening was closing in too, so even the daylight that had filtered through the haze seemed to be steadily losing its strength.

Charlie led them across Cannon Street and they kept going north through the City for what seemed like hours. Meg walked with Flinch, helping her along as she tired. By the time they reached Bishopsgate, Art could feel the ache in his calves and only Jonny seemed able to keep up the pace.

But eventually they arrived at a pair of large wrought-iron gates, set back slightly from the main road. Charlie swung open one of the gates and it screeched on its hinges, crying out for oil. Their feet crunched on unseen gravel and they followed the elderly man's blurred silhouette up a long driveway. Art was surprised that there could be a house with such extensive grounds in the middle of London and he wondered where exactly they were.

The front door opened as soon as they started up the steps. A tall man with an ample stomach restrained by an immaculate suit stared down his nose at them. Art paused, suspecting that the door was about to be slammed shut again. But the man's around face broke into a wide smile. When he spoke, his voice was deep and deferential.

"Welcome home, sir." He turned to survey Art and the other Cannoniers, his smile unfaltering. "I see his lordship has brought some friends with him. Will you be requiring tea, ladies and gentlemen?" He stood aside to let them all troop in after Charlie.

"Tea?" Flinch echoed enthusiastically. Her face was a picture of delight.

"If you wish it, miss," the butler replied with amusement.

"Your lordship?" Meg repeated, saying out loud what Art had been thinking.

Charlie had taken off his hat and jacket and handed them to the butler. "Thank you, Weathers," he murmured. To Art and the others he said, "Please call me Charlie. It's much more friendly, don't you think?"

"More friendly than what?" Jonny asked anxiously.

Charlie shrugged. "Well, to use my full name and title, Charles Etherbridge, Earl of Fotherington."

When the doorbell rang about twenty minutes later, Flinch was already on her third slice of cake. The others sipped at tea served in delicate china cups that Weathers had poured from a large silver teapot.

"That will be your father, Art," Charlie said. He put his cup down on the equally delicate saucer. "I'll just have a quick word with him before we all compare notes, if you don't mind."

Jonny was sitting closest to the door to the hall and he could hear Charlie talking in a low voice. He looked around at the others. Flinch was intent on her tea and cake, grinning happily. Meg seemed bemused, staring down at her empty cup. She was rubbing absentmindedly at her leg. Art was sitting upright, looking anxiously toward the door behind Jonny. He seemed to realize that Jonny was watching him and tried to smile, but his forehead kept its frown lines.

The room was large and square with a high ceiling. Several paintings hung on the walls—large, dark portraits. There were three serious-looking men and a woman who looked as if she were trying not to laugh at them. Jonny wondered if they were relatives or ancestors of Charlie—or "his lordship."

It was difficult to believe that anyone actually lived in the room. Jonny's family living room was a mess of unmatched furniture, his father's books, mother's needle-work, bric-a-brac collected over the years and two tall china dogs either side of the fireplace. There were no china dogs in Charlie's drawing room. There was dark wooden furniture pushed to the walls, large cabinets and a desk.

The tea was set on a tray on the low table in front of them. Jonny was in a large armchair, while Art sat opposite in its twin. Flinch and Meg shared a couch upholstered in deep burgundy material and cluttered with cushions. Charlie had been sitting on a small upright chair.

"Hello, Art."

The voice made Jonny jump. He turned to see Art's father standing just inside the doorway. He was a tall man, broad and well built. He was wearing a rather severe suit that was fading with age, but his expression was kindly and relaxed. He smiled across the room at his son. "Been having fun, I hear."

"You could say that," Art agreed hesitantly.

There was a policeman with Art's dad, and Jonny recognized him as the same constable they had met in the fog earlier.

"If you are in agreement," Charlie was saying as he returned to his chair, "I think Constable Coulson here should let their parents know that Jonny and Meg are all right." He smiled at Jonny. "He can tell them that you're helping the police, and that we're grateful for that and will look after you for the moment. Unless you'd rather he take you home now?"

"I'll stay," Jonny said at once. "But yes, please let Mum and Dad know where I am."

Charlie nodded. "Good. Meg?" he prompted gently.

Meg was looking at the policeman, her face lined with worry. "Make sure you see Mum," she said, her voice husky and quiet. "Dad won't understand." She looked away quickly.

Constable Coulson cleared his throat. "I'll need your addresses," he said. "And what about the other young lady, sir?"

Flinch looked around, obviously wondering who he was talking about. Crumbs of fruitcake dropped from her mouth and landed on her grubby dress.

Charlie smiled. "Don't worry about Miss Flinch. Now, let me ask Weathers to bring Art's father some tea, and then I think we can begin."

It was already dark outside when they started. By the time they finished describing their various adventures it was well after midnight.

Flinch nodded and listened but said almost nothing. Her eyelids were drooping and Art could tell she was tired well before she allowed herself to start yawning. Once she started, it seemed she could not stop, and the girl nestled into Meg beside her on the couch. Soon she was fast asleep, her face blank and free of care.

Charlie had joined Meg and Flinch on the couch, sitting at the opposite end. Art's dad now sat on the upright chair, listening gravely to their story. Occasionally he asked questions, but not once did he seem to discount their version of events or doubt the truth of what they told him.

Art had explained how the Cannoniers had lost their den when Bessemer's exhibition took over. He had suggested that their enquiries about Reggie Yarmouth were motivated by his father's own mention of him being listed as missing, and overhearing some people from the Dog and Goose discussing the mystery. He did not mention the Invisible Detective.

When Jonny talked about how they had sneaked into the exhibition after closing, Art's dad raised an eyebrow.

"It was our den, really," Jonny said.

"So what did you discover?" Art's dad asked.

Meg took up the story, describing how she and Jonny had found the room Art had described, where the mannequins were stored. Then Art told his father and Charlie about Bessemer's strange experiment trying to make the puppet come down the steps. When he described the way that a face had been applied to the other puppet, and how it had walked from the exhibition, the atmosphere in the room seemed to chill.

"He said, 'Good luck, Reggie,'" Art concluded. "I'm sure he did. Just before he saw us."

"And Reggie Yarmouth," Peter Drake said slowly, "has reappeared. With an injured leg that causes him to limp quite badly." He smiled thinly. "You know, if it weren't so absurd and incredible, I might wonder whether the Mr.

Yarmouth I spoke to this afternoon were actually this puppet thing."

Meg gasped. "Of course—that's it."

Art was nodding. "That's what I think."

"It must be," Jonny was muttering. "Must be."

Charlie leaned forward and lifted the teapot experimentally, weighing it to see if there was any tea left. He poured the last dribble of cold liquid into his own cup, then put the teapot down again. "Not as incredible as you might think," he said to Art's dad. "I would have agreed with you entirely a few hours ago. But after what I have seen this evening . . ." He shook his head, sipped at the tea and pulled a face. Then he put the cup down again. "I think, Art, you had better describe to your father what happened that made me decide you might all be safer here with me."

Art nodded. It had not occurred to him until now that Charlie had brought them to his house for protection. But it made sense. If Professor Bessemer knew where their den was, he might also know where they lived.

Again Peter Drake listened attentively. But his expression was now angry more than serious. When Art described how the puppets had cornered him and Meg, his father shook his head and took a deep breath. After Art had finished the story, they all sat in silence. The only sound was Flinch's regular, deep breathing as she slept.

"Well," Charlie said at last, "I think we all agree that Bessemer is intending to replace someone with one of his so-called puppets."

"It seems likely," Art's dad acknowledged. "And I doubt it's Reggie Yarmouth that is his real target. Poor fellow."

He and Charlie were looking at each other as if each knew what the other was thinking. Art could not begin to guess. In his mind he was going over and over what they had heard and seen at the exhibition.

"Maybe it's something to do with the twenty-one steps," he said quietly.

"Maybe," Art's dad replied absently, still looking at Charlie. Then he turned abruptly toward Art. "What did you say?"

"The twenty-one steps. When he was getting the puppet to come down the stairs, he said something about how it had to be able to manage twenty-one steps. I counted them—there *were* twenty-one." He shrugged. "I don't know why."

Charlie was looking closely at Art's dad. "Peter?" he prompted. "Do you know?"

He nodded. "Yes, I think I do." He stood up, walking slowly around behind the chairs and the couch. "There are twenty-one steps in the staircase down from the banqueting hall to the foyer of the Institute of Aeronautical Technology." He paused, looking across the table at Charlie. "Twenty-one steps that the Duke of York has to take down to his official car tomorrow."

"Today," Charlie corrected him. "Tonight, in fact."

"And the institute's valet, the man responsible for helping the duke change after he's made his speech at the dinner and before he comes down those twenty-one steps," Peter Drake said, "is Reggie Yarmouth."

Meg shifted on the couch, carefully moving Flinch so she was more comfortable. "Is the Duke of York important?" she asked.

"He's the king's younger brother, isn't he?" Jonny said.

"That's right," Charlie replied. His expression was graver than Art had yet seen. "And very soon he may possibly become the most important person in the country." He stood up and stretched his shoulders. "If you will excuse me, I think I need to make a telephone call."

"It's after one o'clock in the morning," Art pointed out. "Who's going to answer the phone at this time?"

"The number I'm calling is always answered," Charlie said. "Whatever the hour."

He was gone for several minutes. When he returned, Charlie was once more his usual smiling, avuncular self. "That's all settled," he said, rubbing his hands together. "We can expect a few visitors in the next hour or so. But in the meantime, I have asked Weathers to find beds for Miss Flinch and the other children."

"We'll never get to sleep tonight," Meg protested. But as she spoke, Jonny yawned loudly, which made Charlie and Art's dad laugh. Meg glared.

"Sleep," Art's dad ordered. "We'll let you know what's happening first thing tomorrow when you wake up."

"Aren't we going home?" Jonny asked.

"Not tonight," Charlie said. "Not until this is over and done with, I'm afraid."

Art lingered as Weathers carefully carried the sleeping Flinch from the room, followed reluctantly by Jonny and Meg. "Dad . . . ," he said.

His dad was smiling, as if knowing what he was going to say. "You can stay up," he said. "For now. You're that bit older, and I think our visitor will want to hear firsthand some of the things you've been up to."

"But who is it?" Art wanted to know. "Who do we have to tell about all this?"

"You'll know soon enough," Charlie said. He was standing at the window, pulling back the curtain and peering out into the night.

The cars arrived half an hour later. Big, dark cars, their headlights bathing the curtains with pale yellow light as they swept up the drive and parked at the front of the house. Art joined Charlie and his father at the window and watched them. He counted three cars, visible in the light from the porch and illuminated by each other's headlights.

The two men who got out of the middle car were serious and smart. One of them came to the front door, where Art imagined Weathers was already waiting. Another opened the back door of the car to allow a third man to get out. The third man pulled himself upright, glancing across at the window as he started toward the house. He was wearing a long dark coat over a black waistcoat and pinstriped trousers. He paused when he saw Art and the others watching him, and nodded in greeting.

His face was familiar—craggy and experienced, with oiled black hair and prominent dark eyebrows. Art could remember seeing it several times before. It took him a moment to realize that he was remembering not the face itself but pictures of it. In the newspaper.

It took him another moment to realize who it was. By then the man was entering the room, shaking hands first with Charlie, then with Art's father. "And you are?" the man asked as he reached out to shake Art's hand.

"Art," he said, his voice dry and husky. "Arthur Drake."

"I'm very pleased to meet you, Art," replied the prime minister.

There was not a lot on the "*Real* Invisible Detective" page when it loaded.

> The original Invisible Detective is said to have held consulting sessions in the area of Cannon Street, London, in the 1930s and 1940s. Just as with our website, people put questions to him and he would return with answers the following week. He was called the Invisible Detective, as nobody knew who he really was.

Of course, our Invisible Detective is far more sophisticated—a software package using the latest AI technology and recursive indexing, running on our own dedicated state-of-the-art servers. It uses semantic recognition to parse your questions and then searches its large indexes for websites and links that can answer your enquiry before automatically composing an e-mail reply with that information.

Arthur wasn't sure what any of that actually meant. But it was worth seeing if it worked. So he returned to the main page and typed his question:

Who was Lord Fotherington?

CHAPTER 14

Somehow, describing the bizarre events of the last few days once again made them seem less strange and frightening to Art. He was surprised at the expressions on the faces of the two men with Stanley Baldwin and realized just how restrained the man himself was being. Prompted by Charlie, the prime minister had asked Art to tell him everything and promised not to question or interrupt until he was finished. He was as good as his word.

Art's father had been absent for much of the narrative, returning just as he finished. Baldwin and his two aides asked several questions and got Art to clarify a few things. But they seemed to accept his story at face value.

"There are more things in heaven and earth, young man," the prime minister told Art when he hesitantly questioned this. "More things than you can imagine." Then he turned quickly to Art's father. "What do we know about this Professor Bessemer and his entourage?"

"I've just been checking with the Yard, sir. The girl we know nothing about at all. Crabtree seems to be a sort of factotum—he helps out around the exhibition. Got a record for petty theft several years back, been in a few brawls since." Peter Drake paused before adding, "And he has distant cousins in Austria."

Charlie, the prime minister and the two serious-looking aides all nodded as if this was entirely expected.

"And Bessemer?" Charlie asked. "A German connection perhaps? Or possibly Russian?"

Drake nodded. "Absolutely. He seems to have some sort of qualification from the University of Munich, though he isn't listed as a professor there. That's a sort of trade name. Arrived at Dover three months ago with his paraphernalia. Customs flagged him, of course, and he's on the internment list just in case . . . you know."

Again everyone nodded.

Art steeled himself and said, "I don't know."

They all turned to look at him.

"Sorry." He shrugged. "But if I had some idea what you're all talking about, I might be able to help."

"Need to know," one of the aides barked.

But Baldwin gestured for him to be quiet. "As I'm sure you are aware," he said to Art, "Herr Hitler is rearming Germany and in March he reoccupied the Rhineland. Of course, we all hope and pray that his intention is merely to take back what he believes belongs to Germany. But while we may *hope* that, I am beginning to realize that we must prepare for the worst."

"You think Bessemer may be a German spy?"

"It seems likely," Charlie said.

"But what's he doing? I mean, it's not like he's listening at keyholes or trying to sabotage airplanes or anything, is he?"

Baldwin's forehead lined with concentration and Art guessed he was thinking how best to phrase what he had to tell them. "As you know, we have a new king," he said at last. "But you will not know that before long, perhaps this year even, we may have *another* new king."

Art gasped.

"Is his majesty ill?" his father asked.

Baldwin smiled thinly. "Some might say so. But no, not really. His majesty," he said simply, "is in love."

"I've heard the rumors about this American woman," Drake said. "But is that a problem?"

"In this case, yes, it is. You see, this is a woman who has recently divorced her second husband. A most unsuitable candidate, not just in my opinion, which I am sure I shall soon be asked, but in the opinions of just about everyone who matters." He sat back in the chair, his hands still clasped tightly together. "Of course, the king may come to his senses. But equally, and I know his majesty quite well, he may decide that giving up his throne is a small price to pay in order to be with the woman he loves."

There was silence in the room. Even to Art this was shattering news, and he could see that his father's face was drained of color.

"The king has no children," his father said. "If he should . . . abdicate"—he glanced at Baldwin, as if unsure whether he was allowed even to say the word—"then he would be succeeded by his younger brother."

Now Art could see the connection. "The Duke of York," he breathed.

Charlie was holding a drink out to Art's father. A cut-glass tumbler, the facets catching the light. It looked like whisky and Art could hear the clink of ice. "It seems," Charlie said, "that Professor Bessemer may be anticipating events. Rather than try to replace the king with one of his puppet creatures, the Duke of York is an altogether easier target."

"But would he know of this crisis?" Art's father asked, sipping at the drink.

"It is possible," Baldwin admitted. "Probable even. In this country Lord Beaverbrook has managed to keep speculation out of the papers, but there are certainly rumors abroad, as it were." He looked up at Charlie. "I think I might partake as well, Charles. If you have sufficient whisky."

"Of course."

"So Bessemer replaces the Duke of York with one of his mannequin things," Art said. "Then when the duke becomes king . . ."

"He has in his control what we might call a puppet monarchy," Baldwin agreed. "One that is presumably sympathetic to German expansionism." He took the drink that Charlie offered and sipped at it.

"But what if the crisis comes to nothing?" Art's dad wanted to know.

"That is a risk, of course. But in the worst case, from their point of view, they have an agent placed very close to the king. And for all the power of his majesty's government, politicians come and go, but the king is a more permanent fixture in uncertain times."

"So," Charlie said, "what do we do?"

"What indeed?" the prime minister wondered.

There was a hushed silence in the room, broken only by Art's loud yawn.

"I think it's time you got some sleep," Art's dad whispered.

Charlie was standing beside Art now and gestured for him to get up. "Weathers will show you to a room," he said quietly. "You've done so much, but you can leave the rest to us now. It's in the best possible hands."

As Art got up to leave, the prime minister stood up too. Once again, he shook Art's hand. "Thank you, young man," he said. "Thank you so very much. I am afraid that in the years ahead, we will need many more brave young men like yourself if we are to survive the gathering storm."

Art was asleep almost as soon as he was in bed. He did not bother to get undressed, and anyway he had no pajamas. Weathers had quietly shown him into a room with two single beds and Art could hear Jonny breathing heavily in his sleep in the other bed.

He dreamed of things he did not understand: of friends and a school he did not know, of machines that threw images and text onto a glass screen . . . When he did eventually awaken, with the sunlight streaming through a gap between the curtains and the wall, Jonny was already sitting up in bed, fully dressed and looking around, confused.

There was a washbasin in the corner of the room and fresh towels over the ends of their beds. As they washed, Art quickly told Jonny what had happened the previous evening after he went to bed.

"You're kidding," Jonny said. "The prime minister."

Art nodded. "Really." He lowered his voice, worried that someone might overhear. "And what he said is really secret, all right?"

Jonny nodded, his eyes wide.

"I mean *really*," Art emphasized. Then he told Jonny in a hushed voice about the king and the woman he loved, and what Bessemer was planning.

"So what do we do?" Jonny asked when Art had finished his story.

"We leave it to Mr. Baldwin to sort out Bessemer. Those two men with him," Art went on, still talking quietly as they sat side by side on one of the beds, "I'm sure they're with the secret service."

Jonny nodded. "Seems likely," he agreed.

"It's Liza I'm worried about," Art confessed. "What will happen to her once Bessemer . . ."

"Perhaps she has family."

"Perhaps," Art said. "But she hasn't mentioned it. She seemed to need to escape." He bit at his bottom lip as he considered. "I think we need to get her away from the exhibition, just in case Bessemer makes his way back there. If something goes wrong." He paused, wondering if he should tell Jonny what he had agreed with Liza the previous day—that he had said he would meet her at the exhibition tonight and take her away, save her from Bessemer.

"Jonny," Art said at last, "can you keep a secret?"

"Of course I can." He sounded put out that Art had to ask.

But before Art could apologize and tell Jonny about his meeting with Liza, they both heard the scream.

"Flinch!" said Art at once.

"What are they doing to her?" Jonny shouted above the continued yells as they wrenched open the door and tore down the corridor outside.

Art's face was set, his teeth gritted. "We'll soon find out," he shouted back.

The reply was there on Sunday morning when Arthur checked. The time stamp on the e-mail said it had been sent at 10:17 the previous night, and the e-mail was from <u>BrandonLake@Invisible-Detective.com</u>.

The text was short. It was basically a form letter that thanked Arthur for using the services of the Invisible Detective and apologized that only one relevant link had been found.

The link took him to a page about British prime ministers

of the twentieth century. There was a lot on the page, text and pictures. Arthur scrolled right through without seeing a reference to Lord Fotherington. He tried "Find (on this page) . . ." from the menu, and the window jumped to a picture. The word "Fotherington" in the caption was backlit:

> Stanley Baldwin (left) pictured with Lord Fotherington shortly before Baldwin's retirement in 1937.

Arthur peered at the grainy black-and-white picture. It was slightly out of focus, but even without the caption he would have recognized both Baldwin and Fotherington.

Which scared him. Because while they were both as familiar as old family photos, he had never seen a picture of either of them before in his life.

CHAPTER 15

Flinch escaped before they got there. She appeared at the end of the corridor, wrapped in a white towel. Her hair was dripping wet and her face was soaked in tears and soapy water.

"A bath!" she shrieked at Art and Jonny as they raced up to her. "They were giving me a bath!" Then she collapsed in an angry heap, the towel spreading around her like a puddle.

Jonny and Art just stared. The towel was huge and covered the whole of Flinch's body as she huddled inside, holding it tightly about her. Just her head was visible, her face crumpled into annoyance. But her skin was pale and pink rather than grubby and ingrained with dirt. Her hair was already beginning to dry to a golden blond in place of the usual dull brown.

The door behind Flinch opened again and a large matronly woman wearing an apron emerged. She was almost as wet as Flinch, though she seemed amused rather than upset.

"Now come along, miss," the woman said in a kindly voice. "It's all over now. And Mr. Weathers has had your clothes washed and pressed, ready for you. Let's just get your hair dry, shall we?"

The towel around Flinch rose and fell as she harrumphed in annoyance and turned away. "A bath," she said again, shaking her head, as if she could still not quite believe the misfortune she had suffered so cruelly at this woman's hands.

Art crouched down beside Flinch and smiled awkwardly. "I think you'd better let her dry your hair and get you dressed," he said. Flinch looked at him as if he was mad, so Art quickly went on, "After all, it must be nearly time for breakfast."

The girl's eyes narrowed, and she glanced quickly at the woman, then back at Art.

The woman had seen her look and caught on immediately. "Oh, dear me, yes," she said. "There'll be toast and marmalade and bacon and eggs . . ."

"Bacon?" Flinch struggled to her feet, the towel still tight around her as she shuffled back toward the bathroom. A shallow pool of water was emerging from under the door.

"And maybe even devils on horseback," the woman went on as she opened the door again to let Flinch through.

Art and Jonny caught a glimpse of the dripping walls, and a sodden pile of towels beside a huge enameled bath before they both turned away.

"What are devils on horseback?" Flinch was asking with polite interest as the door closed and she disappeared from sight.

Despite the cautions and warnings, the Cannoniers had no intention of leaving everything to the proper authorities.

They would certainly be on hand to watch if not actually supervise events that evening. There was no discussion or heart-searching about it. Art suggested they meet at eight o'clock and the others nodded in agreement.

Art's biggest worry was the timing. Nobody had seemed to know how long the dinner at the institute would go on, or for how long the Duke of York intended to speak afterward. With luck it would be over by half-past nine at the latest. After that, Art had decided, he would leave the others to it and keep his appointment with Liza.

There was no way he could let the girl down. In his mind's eye, he could see her round, delicate face with the full lips and huge appealing eyes as she looked up at him. He could remember every detail of her rolling, stumbling walk as she shuffled back to the exhibition after their discussion on Cannon Street. He could imagine putting his arm around her shoulder and leading her away from the old warehouse, along the street to a better life away from Bessemer and Creepy Crabtree.

So when they heard the city clocks chiming the half hour and there was still no sign of the duke, Art whispered to Jonny that it was time for him to go and then slipped away before Meg or Flinch noticed. He had told Jonny what was happening, and he was sure the Cannoniers could manage without him. They would meet later for a full report of what happened at the institute. Liza would be there, grateful and surprised by the events that were about to unfold.

It was with excitement and anticipation rather than anxiety and nervousness that Art made his way quickly down the road toward the river, toward Bessemer's Paranormal Puppets.

The speech went well. The duke was not a natural speaker and, unlike his brother, did not relish appearing in public. But he managed to control his nerves, and the audience smiled and laughed and clapped appreciatively in the places where he had been told they would.

It was with a mixture of relief and anticipation that he left the dinner. The other diners were staying for coffee and liqueurs, but he had closed his speech by apologizing for the fact that he had to go. Although he was already behind schedule, the worst of the day was over now.

He made his way across the landing to the paneled room where he had been told the institute's valet would be waiting to help him into his coat. Quite why it was necessary for anyone to help him, the duke was not sure, but he was not the type of man to make a fuss.

There were two men in the room. One was the valet, standing stiffly beside the large wooden table. As soon as the duke closed the door, the valet shuffled over in his strange limping manner. His moustache twitched and he flicked at it with his hand—an odd, almost furtive gesture. His other hand was in his jacket pocket.

The duke's attention, however, was on the second figure. There was something familiar about the man. He was about the same height and build as the duke himself. Like the duke, he was wearing a dark suit. An identical suit now that he came to look more closely. The man was turned away, so the duke could not see his face.

"What's going on, Yarmouth?" the duke asked. His confusion turned quickly to anger and fear as the valet's hand emerged from his jacket pocket—holding a revolver.

The duke took a step backward. Several things now happened at once. The valet—Yarmouth—raised the revolver and aimed it directly at the duke. The man in the identical suit turned, and the duke could see his face. Or rather, he could see that there was no face, just a crude pale lump of flesh—the hint of a bump for a nose and dark indentations for eyes.

And as the faceless figure stepped toward him, a section of the paneling behind it swung slowly open to allow a third figure to step into the room.

Meg's feet were tired. She had been standing for so long that she had pins and needles and could feel the muscles in her calves protesting. For over an hour she had been focusing her attention on the main door to the Institute of Aeronautical Technology.

The Cannoniers were hiding at the next corner. They had a good view of both the institute itself and the duke's official car waiting outside. Further along the street, on the opposite side of the road to the institute, another car was parked—a large black car with two shadowy figures just visible inside. The man in the driving seat was undoubtedly Bessemer. Meg had seen his profile clearly as he leaned across at one point to talk to his companion. Creepy Crabtree no doubt, Art had said.

It was almost quarter to ten and the evening was turning to dusk. Thin clouds mottled the darkening summer sky. Flinch was sitting cross-legged on the pavement, obviously not at all worried about getting her clothes dirty again. Jonny was shuffling nervously beside Meg. And Art . . .

She turned to see what Art was doing. He was not there. Meg could feel something close to panic in the pit of her stomach as she looked further along the street, then back at the car. From where they were concealed, several uniformed policemen were visible, all as alert and attentive as the Cannoniers themselves. But there was no sign of Art.

Jonny saw Meg looking around and quickly avoided her gaze, looking down at his feet.

"Where is he?" she demanded. Jonny did not answer. "I can tell you know where he is," she said, her voice shrill with anger and concern.

So Jonny told her. Flinch pulled herself to her feet to listen. "Will Liza be a Cannonier?" she asked as Jonny finished.

"No," Meg snapped immediately. "No she will not. The fool." She was in two minds as to whether to stay with Jonny and Flinch or to follow Art.

"I don't see what the problem is," Jonny protested.

Meg glared at him and he fell silent. But before Meg could answer, Flinch tugged at her sleeve.

"Look." She was pointing toward the institute.

The door was opening. There was a figure framed with the light behind. A silhouette of a man in a suit and a long dark coat. He wore a top hat pulled down low so that the brim shaded his eyes, and as Meg watched he took an uncertain, halting step forward, toward the official car.

Meg glanced over at the other car. The door was open, and the tall, thin figure of Bessemer was standing, looking across the street.

The shuffling figure continued its hesitant, limping progress toward the official car. For the briefest moment, it seemed to look up, glancing across at Bessemer, as if to reassure itself that he was there.

The warehouse was in darkness. Art was too big to fit through the window at the back where Flinch could squeeze in, even if he could reach it. Instead, after listening for a while and hearing nothing, he decided that the direct and obvious approach was best. Liza was expecting him and he knew Bessemer was not there, so he knocked loudly on the main door.

Whether it was fear or prudence, he was not sure, but after he knocked, Art ran to the corner of the building. He angled himself so he could see the door, but could not easily be seen himself. After perhaps a minute, the door was opened and a figure looked out. Seeing nobody, the figure stepped into the street and stared around.

But it was not Liza. It was Old Creepy Crabtree. The caretaker's bent silhouette was easily recognizable against the gathering gloom. "Who's there?" he called suspiciously.

When there was no reply, he walked slowly to the end of the warehouse—the opposite end to where Art was hiding.

Without thinking, Art ran quickly to the open door and slipped inside. Where was Liza? Was Crabtree keeping her a prisoner there while Bessemer and another accomplice were at the institute? Art slammed the door shut and turned the key. There was a heavy wooden locking bar, but Art resisted the temptation to slide it home.

For a moment the scene was frozen like one of the strange displays in Bessemer's exhibition.

Meg watched with startled realization. Jonny was gaping beside her and Flinch clutched at Meg's arm. The figure that had emerged from the institute stared across at Bessemer, who was gazing coldly back. Bessemer's accomplice stood beside him at the curb.

Then with a speed and fluidity that belied his earlier jerky movements, the figure by the official car put his hand to his mouth. The shrill sound of the police whistle blasted across the street. Immediately, Bessemer stiffened. His companion struggled to get back into the car, but the thin professor was running around, grabbing his accomplice, dragging and pulling them away from the car—away from the group of policemen running toward them.

The man from the institute, the man with the whistle, was running across the street. His hat came off and his coat flapped open as he raced toward Bessemer, and Meg could see now that it was Art's father. His face was set in an expression of grim satisfaction.

The place seemed deserted. The last room Art tried was the storeroom. The life-sized puppets stared at him disconcertingly as he opened the door and peered inside.

"Liza?"

No answer. He was about to close the door again when he caught sight of the display cabinet on the wall. Inside the strange pebble seemed to glow with inner light and Art recalled how emphatic Liza had been about getting back her "stone."

He crossed the room quickly and pulled open the cabinet. He reached inside and lifted the stone from its shelf.

It was difficult to see exactly what was happening. Meg and Jonny both stepped out from their hiding places to get a better view. Flinch pushed between them, wriggling her shoulders.

The police were converging on Bessemer from all directions now. Officers had appeared from side streets and doorways. Sergeant Drake was shouting above the noise and confusion.

Meg caught a single word: "Gun!"

And she could see it. Bessemer was holding a large pistol. It was about the size of a revolver, but flat with no visible chambers. She caught just a glimpse of it before Drake's hand chopped down at Bessemer's wrist. The gun clattered to the ground and a mass of dark blue surged over the struggling professor.

From the confusion, a single small figure in a scarlet, fur-trimmed coat lurched free. She limped away from the struggling group, the braces on her legs clearly visible as she struggled and stumbled along the pavement.

Liza.

Toward where the gun had fallen. She balanced herself, feet apart, before awkwardly scooping up the pistol and turning. The fight was all but over now. Bessemer was held by his arms, spread-eagled across a wall of uniforms. Sergeant Drake stood beside him, fumbling with handcuffs.

Then Bessemer was pointing, his stubbed-off finger jabbing through the air toward where Liza was leveling the gun. He was shouting, but his words did not carry as far as Meg and the others.

And their ears were ringing with the noise of the shot. An explosion of sound echoed off the buildings. The police struggled and staggered under the dead weight they now held. Drake was lying on the ground, trying to disentangle himself from the mass of arms and legs as Bessemer's body crashed down, bringing several policemen with him.

The professor seemed to be staring across at Liza. One

hand was still outstretched, pointing, clutching, dying. Then his head lolled away and Meg closed her eyes to avoid seeing the blood.

When she opened them again, they were dragging Bessemer's body away. Liza was gone.

"It's time to go, if you're interested."

Arthur caught his breath in surprise. "Dad, you made me jump."

His dad was leaning over his shoulder, reading the text in the window. "Stanley Baldwin, eh? Thought it was medieval stuff this term."

"It's the Victorians," Arthur told him. "Medieval stuff was ages ago."

Dad looked at him, and they both laughed at that.

"Whatever," Dad said at last. "Anyway, I'm off. You decided if you're coming to see Gramps this time?"

Arthur tried not to shudder at the thought. He liked his grandad. He had fond memories of sitting on the old man's knee a long time ago and walking in the park—kicking a football even. But he couldn't face the home. It made him feel embarrassed, like he was intruding.

"I want to read up on the abdication crisis," he said, turning back to the screen. "Edward VIII, you know."

"Gramps would know. You can ask him." Dad put his

hand on Arthur's shoulder. "It's all right, you stay here. I know you don't like coming."

"It's not that, Dad. I love Grandad, really I do. But . . ."

"I know you do." The hand lifted. "You sort out some dinner for us. And don't spend too long on that. Someone has to pay the phone bill, you know."

"Thanks, Dad." He turned around in the chair. "I'll come next time. Promise."

Dad was at the door. "OK," he said. "I'll hold you to that, mind."

"Fair enough."

Arthur disconnected from the Internet as soon as the door closed. He could hear his dad collecting his keys and loose change from his bedside cabinet. It was only when Art went to close the e-mail program that he saw another message had arrived while he had been connected. Another message from the Invisible Detective.

CHAPTER 16

Art was staring deep into the swirling vortex patterns of the strange stone, but the gunshot sound of the main door slamming shut broke the spell. He slipped the stone into his pocket and ran quickly from the room.

If, again, the heads of the life-sized puppets arranged in the center of the room angled to watch his departure, he did not notice.

Liza was walking through the exhibition as quickly as she could manage. She stopped when she saw Art and waited for him to reach her. She was standing beside the painted park, where the dog still jumped but the boy and his ball were gone. She was huddled inside her large red coat with its white fur collar. Her arms were folded across her chest, her hands pushed inside the cuffs of the opposite sleeves.

"You have the stone," she said as Art approached. It was not a question, but he nodded. "We must go." She turned awkwardly back toward the entrance.

"There's no hurry," he said as he caught her up. "The professor won't find us."

He was going to explain, but she said, "I know. But we must still hurry."

"Don't you have any bags? Any luggage?" He was walking beside her now, past the steps up to the priestless coronation. He spared the queen a glance and she gazed glassily back at him.

"You have the stone," Liza repeated. She stopped and looked up at Art. She pulled her hands out of the sleeves and raised her left hand. The tips of her fingers brushed against his cheek. They seemed cold. "Thank you. You have set me free."

Art felt himself begin to redden. "Well, not yet. We still have to get out of here." He stopped as a thought struck him. "How did you get past Old Creepy? He was outside, I locked him out."

"Why do you call him creepy?"

Art shrugged. "Because he is."

"He wasn't there." She took another lurching step forward. "He must have gone. I locked the door again behind me."

Art took Liza's arm, helping her balance as they made their ponderous way along the aisle.

It had taken them several minutes to get over the shock. Flinch was crying into Meg's chest. Jonny just stared in horror at the scene in front of them. They watched as an ambulance arrived and Bessemer's body was taken away.

It was perhaps ten minutes before Meg suddenly exclaimed, "Art!"

Flinch pulled away, sensing Meg's tension.

"He'll be all right. He was long gone," Jonny told them.

"Think," Meg ordered. "Where did you say he was going?"

"Well," Jonny said defensively, "I told you. He's gone . . ." He stopped, feeling the color drain from his face.

"What is it?" Flinch asked, looking from Jonny to Meg.

"He's gone to the exhibition," Meg said quietly, her voice full of nerves and anger. "He's gone to meet Liza."

"But—Liza . . ." Flinch was frowning with concentration. "She just shot Bessemer."

"Flinch, wait here," Meg ordered. "I'll get Art's dad. And Charlie."

"What shall I do?" Jonny asked.

Meg stared at him. "Run!" she hissed.

Jonny ran. He ran as he had never run before. He ran till his chest ached with the pressure and he could hardly breathe and the pavement was a blur under his feet as the night began to close in, and still he ran.

When he reached the exhibition, he went straight to the main doors. Was he here before Liza? He was quick, far quicker than she was, but the crippled girl had a long start on him. The doors were locked. They were heavy and wooden, and there was no way Jonny would be able to break in that way. He stepped back, breathing deeply, his lungs aching with the effort. His feet caught on something on the ground behind him, something he had not seen in the thickening darkness, and he nearly fell.

Jonny stood staring down, his hands on his knees and the blood rushing in his ears. On the ground at his feet was the curled, motionless body of Old Creepy Crabtree.

They stopped as soon as the hammering on the door began again.

"Old Creepy's come back," Art whispered.

"Or someone else," Liza suggested.

"Who?"

She did not answer. They turned and started down the aisle, toward the back of the warehouse. Art looked at Liza as they walked slowly together. He could see every strand of her ink-black hair, every pore on her perfect face. Every fiber of white fur on her collar as it rippled with the breeze as they walked. And in among the mass of white there were flecks of red. Scarlet. Matching the color of the rest of her coat. Splashes of dye? Not that it mattered. It was as if he was staring into the strange stone again, feeling its influence flow through him. Nothing mattered now, Art realized, as they walked slowly along the main aisle through the exhibition, past the paranormal puppets.

And as they went, each and every inhuman head slowly turned to watch their progress.

Hammering on the door was doing no good. All he was likely to achieve, Jonny decided, was to attract the attention of the violent lady with the brush across the street. There was the back door, but he doubted he'd have any more luck there. Perhaps Art wasn't there. Perhaps Liza hadn't yet arrived. His mind ran through the possibilities as quickly as his feet had brought him here.

But always he came back to two images: Bessemer collapsing to the ground as Liza fired the gun, and the prone body of Old Creepy lying at his feet. The man seemed to be breathing and he had a lump on his head. A lump that was sticky to the touch and left a dark stain on Jonny's fingers when he felt around it.

A footfall along the pavement startled him and he jumped back. A figure was looming out of the hazy darkness. It solidified into the shape of a girl.

"Jonny?"

"Flinch!" He shook his head with relief. "Meg told you to stay put."

"I did. But she took forever. And I didn't think you'd be able to get in."

Jonny smiled at her to show he wasn't angry, just startled. "You got that right. It's all locked up."

"Come on, then," she said, and Flinch led him around to the back of the warehouse.

It was very dark inside. Flinch could see the glimmerings of light from the lower floor as she tumbled in through the upstairs window. The door to the small room was open and she ran quickly and quietly to the stairs beyond. Jonny would be waiting at the door. She listened carefully for a moment and thought she could hear voices. Was it Art? Let

Jonny in first, she decided, then they could both look for Art.

There was a puppet at the bottom of the stairs. It had not been there before. It was standing silent and still between the stairs and the back door of the warehouse. It was a figure of a man, dressed in working clothes like a dockhand or a market porter. Flinch spared the figure a glance, taking in its unfinished lumpy face as she edged around toward the door.

It was the glance that saved her.

The figure's head was swinging slowly around, as if it was watching Flinch. Instinctively Flinch jumped back— just as the figure's arm lashed out, its fingers clutching the air where Flinch's throat had so recently been.

She gave a squeal of terror and half heard Jonny's muffled shouts from behind the door.

The puppet took a lurching step toward her as she backed away. Her back hit the wall and she started to edge along, toward the stairs. Maybe this one couldn't climb stairs. It was lumbering uncertainly toward her now, rocking from side to side as it moved. She could outrun it easily, if she had the room.

There was a thud from the door and it trembled. Jonny was trying to smash it down, kicking at it maybe. Flinch was at the bottom of the stairs. The puppet paused, as if daring her to escape. There was something odd about the way it stood, arms outstretched and fingers snapping together like jaws, watching her through its sightless eyes.

Flinch looked up the stairs—did it want her to try to escape that way? Sure enough, in the shadows at the top landing she could just make out another figure waiting for her.

The door shuddered again under an outside impact, and splinters of wood tore away from it. Flinch leaned toward the stairs, as if about to run up them. The puppet took another step toward her, arms reaching like a sleepwalker. The fingers were almost within reach of Flinch now.

Hoping it looked like she was about to run, Flinch ducked back the other way. She grabbed one of the puppet's hands in both her own, squeezing the trembling fingers together, and pushed as hard as she could.

The puppet rocked backward on its heels, stumbling as it lost its balance. It teetered around as it tried to save itself from falling. Flinch was long past it, at the door, shouting to Jonny, scrabbling at the bolt.

But the door had shifted on its hinges under Jonny's assault and the bolt was hard against the socket, unmoving. Flinch tore at it till her nails were shredded. Behind her she could hear the heavy tread of the puppet, she could imagine the second figure lurching down the stairs toward her. Her eyes stung with salt tears and she dared not look around, dared not stop fighting the bolt, dared not fail her friends.

Suddenly the bolt shot back, catching her hand on the way and making her shriek with pain as the skin was pinched and bruised. She jumped aside as the door crashed open. She stared at her injured hand as the door caught the puppet that had been right behind her and sent it reeling into the other inhuman figure that was lurching across from the stairs. The two of them staggered and fell.

"Are you all right?" Jonny gasped as he leaped through the door.

"The bolt left dents on my hand," Flinch told him in surprise. "Look." She held her hand up for him to see.

Jonny pushed it aside. "Show me later. We have to find Art." He was staring at the flailing puppets as they struggled to pull themselves up. He grabbed her by the wrist and pulled her toward the main exhibition hall.

"Well done, Flinch," he said as they ran, still holding hands, and she grinned.

Flinch stopped grinning as they burst through the doors into the main exhibition area. They emerged beside the pub scene and, as soon as they were on the main aisle, Flinch could see Art.

He was walking slowly toward them, holding Liza's arm and helping her along. Flinch and Jonny skidded to a halt.

"Jonny—what's going on?" Art demanded. His face was a mask of bewilderment and surprise.

Liza had stopped walking and held him back.

Before Jonny could reply, there was a tremendous crash from the front of the warehouse. A splintering and wrenching that could only be the main doors being torn open.

Then running feet, and moments later Art's father and Meg appeared at the other end of the aisle. Charlie was visible behind them, breathless as he struggled to keep up.

"What is this?" Art asked, confused.

More movement. The figures in the pub were slowly stirring into life. They swayed uncertainly, as if in a strong breeze, before lurching forward and spilling into the aisle between Flinch and Art. One of the women, her face a painted mess, casually lashed out and smashed the glass she held on the edge of the bar. Splintered remains in front of her like a knife, she stalked toward Flinch and Jonny.

Through the crowding figures, Flinch could see Art climbing the first few steps toward the queen, looking over the heads of the puppets to see what was happening. Liza was still at the bottom of the steps, lost now to Flinch's sight.

But she could hear Meg shouting.

Art struggled to see over the heads of the shuffling figures that were filling the aisle either side of himself and Liza. Jonny and Flinch were trapped behind the customers from the pub, while his dad, Meg and Charlie were held back by both executioner and victim—united now in a common cause. The masked executioner hefted a lethal-looking ax, while his previously intended victim had a wooden stake torn from the scenery wall.

"Art!" Meg was shouting. "Art—get away from her!"

Art looked down at Liza. Her huge eyes met his gaze.

"She's doing this, can't you see that?" Meg's voice was shrill.

"Meg's right." It was his dad calling now. From his vantage point on the steps, Art could see the three of them backing away from the executioner's swinging ax. In his pocket, his hand was tight about the stone from the display case.

"It's not her," Art shouted back. "Not Liza. It can't be." He was looking around for some explanation, any explanation. "It must be Bessemer, he still controls them somehow."

"Bessemer's dead." It was Charlie shouting now. His voice was cracked and hoarse. "She shot him, do you hear me? Liza shot him dead."

Art gasped. "Liza?"

"I had to," she said levelly. She took a faltering, difficult first step onto the staircase. "I had to get away." She staggered dangerously as she made the second step. "You have to believe me, Art. If you knew what he was like, what he did, how he controlled . . . everything."

"Art—get away from her!"

"Creepy Crabtree, then," Art shouted back at Jonny. "It must be Old Creepy. He was here earlier, then he left."

"He didn't leave." Jonny's voice was barely audible above the rushing in his ears. "He's out cold. She hit him with something."

"Is that true?" Art hissed at Liza. He did not know what to think, whom to believe, what to do.

Liza was shaking her head. "Of course not, Art." The third step. She staggered, almost slipped and instinctively he grabbed her wrist and helped her keep her footing. "I just want to be with you, Art, that's all." She was standing next to him now. Her face was close to his, her eyes locked on his own.

Meg's voice was ringing in Art's ears. "She's lying," Meg shouted, ducking beneath the swinging ax. "Can't you tell she's lying? Believe me—I know."

"She knows nothing," Liza countered. Her voice was soft and quiet. Reasonable and calm. "I love you, Art," she breathed.

Art stared back. At the edges of his vision he could see Flinch and Jonny backing away from the woman with the glass; his dad and Charlie wrestling with another figure; Meg jumping clear of the executioner's ax. But it was Liza's china-perfect face that filled his thoughts.

Arthur sat frozen in the chair, staring at the screen. All his attention was focused on the single line of text in the message from BrandonLake@Invisible-Detective.com. Just six words. He read it a third time, wondering if it was worth the has-

sle of connecting again. Or was it simply an advert or a gim-
mick of some sort? He got enough of that in his e-mail.

The message said:

> Ask me about the Shadow Beast.

Arthur was brought back to reality by the sound of the
front door banging shut. He blinked and came to a sudden
decision. The window above the computer looked out of the
front of the house and he leaned across and opened it. Outside he could see his dad unlocking the car.

"Hang on, Dad," Arthur shouted.

His father looked up, startled.

"I'm coming with you," Arthur called.

Arthur's grandfather had his own small room in the home. It
was one of scores of identical rooms with impersonal name-
plates off hospital-green corridors. Arthur didn't like it. He
felt embarrassed going there because he was sure that his
grandad didn't like it either. But he was too old and frail to
stay at home. After his third fall in as many months, it was
obvious he needed someone close at hand, however much
he might value his independence.

"It's a shock for him," Arthur remembered his dad telling
him once. "He was so independent. Even after my mum died,
he wouldn't have any help. Had to do everything himself."

It was a shock to Arthur too. He could understand if
someone was ill. But getting old was different—it was like

being ill, except you knew you were never going to get better. It wasn't that he looked at Grandad and saw himself in seventy years' time—that was so far in the future he could make no connection. But he could see from the way his grandad looked back at him that he was remembering what it was like to be younger, that he had once been a teenager. . . .

"Arthur's doing some research into family trees or something," Dad said as soon as they'd settled themselves. There were only two chairs—a small armchair and an upright chair at a small desk Grandad had brought with him. So Arthur sat on the bed. "It's for school," Dad explained.

Grandad turned to look at Arthur. His eyes were still bright and alert. "Is that so?" He smiled, his face cracking into a mass of wrinkles. "For school?"

Arthur shifted uncomfortably. He felt the covers scrunching under him. "Well . . . I'm interested." He looked away, pretending to be absorbed in the half-completed crossword in the folded newspaper on the bedside cabinet.

"It's good to be interested in things," Grandad observed, nodding slowly. "Especially when you get to my time of life. History, reading, doing the crossword." He waved vaguely in the direction of the bedside cabinet. "Curious old notebooks," he added.

CHAPTER 17

The stone was tight in Art's hand, fitting perfectly into his palm. His other hand still held Liza's wrist, helping her balance on the step.

"Ever since I first saw you," Liza said, "I could feel the strength of your will. It is even stronger now. Such control. That's how you freed me from Bessemer. Now you have the lodestone, you've set me free from him."

"You shot Bessemer," Art said slowly, unable to believe it.

"I had to break his hold on me." Her eyes were still locked on his. "Don't you see that?"

There was a loud crash and Art snapped back to reality, breaking away from her gaze and turning instinctively toward the sound. Art's father had grabbed the executioner's ax and pushed the large figure roughly away. The sound was the ax falling to the floor as the executioner's arms windmilled and he tried to stay upright. He tottered, staggered and then collapsed to the floor beside the fallen ax. Moments later, the second puppet from the tableau followed as Peter Drake shoved it violently across the aisle.

Without thinking, Art took his hand from Liza's wrist, hardly noticing as she tried to grab it back.

"No," she hissed. Then louder, shouting down at Art's dad: "No—he's mine!"

Art's dad was walking calmly toward the steps. He ignored the grotesque group of customers from the pub who were swinging away from Jonny and Flinch and shuffling menacingly back to block his progress. His eyes were fixed on Art—reassuring, but tinged with sadness.

"Time to go, Art," he said again, gently.

Movement to Art's side. He saw his father freeze in midstep. Glancing toward Liza, he saw the gun as it emerged from her pocket and swung toward his father. Saw her wide eyes fix on him, her elegant finger tighten on the trigger and the gun move so slightly with the pressure. Reality slowed.

The only thing moving in real time was Art's arm as he lashed out. His fist connected with the pistol as it fired. Even the sound was blurred as the shot went wide and splinters flew from the wall beyond Meg and Charlie. Both ducked at the sound, but Art's dad did not move.

Charlie was back on his feet, moving quickly forward, hand inside his jacket.

Art's dad stood absolutely still, while the woman with the broken glass lurched threateningly toward him.

Liza was turning back toward Art, her eyes wide in anger and astonishment, the gun coming up again. Then suddenly she was flinging herself forward. The metal cages on her legs rasped together as she hurled herself toward him.

The gun jabbed into his ribs and her other arm closed

around his neck. He could not move as she embraced him tight. He waited, frozen, for the shot that would tear out his heart.

The sound of the gun echoed around the exhibition. For a second Art felt nothing. Empty. Dead.

Then the pressure was gone from his chest. The grip on his neck slackened. Charlie was standing at the bottom of the steps beside Art's father. A curl of smoke wisped from the end of the revolver he held. Art's view was obscured by Liza as she fell back from him, tumbling down the steps. She made no effort to break her fall, no movement whatsoever. It was like watching a doll being dropped down stairs.

One by one the figures from the pub scene buckled and fell. Their legs gave way beneath the weight of their bodies and they collapsed, lifeless. Puppets with no strings.

Liza landed on her back, angled so she was looking back up at Art. The bullet had torn into her head, shattering her delicate features. Art could see clearly the sharp edges where the face had broken like eggshell. He could see the dark hollow interior. The side of her face was gone— one cheek and an eye replaced by the ragged hole. The other side of her face was still as perfect as ever. A single eye stared glassily up at Art through impossibly long lashes, out of a shattered porcelain face. Then the lifeless body slipped down further, the head lolled to one side and the eye slowly closed. As the head rolled back, the eye opened once more for an instant before closing again. Like a doll when you lay it down to sleep.

• • •

The room was silent save for the whisper of the curtains as the breeze caught them. The crowd pressed into the tight space waited with anticipation. The Invisible Detective was about to speak.

If his voice seemed a little strained this Monday evening, then only Meg, Jonny and Flinch, hiding behind the curtain, noticed. Meg frowned at Jonny and gestured for him to be careful with his fishing rod. Flinch smiled at them both, bouncing lightly on her feet with her usual excitement.

"Several weeks ago," Brandon Lake's voice said, "I was asked about missing people. In particular, at that time, about Reggie Yarmouth." The Invisible Detective paused, as if uncertain how to continue. "I have to tell you," he continued after a while, "that while we shall, sadly, not see Reggie and the others again, there will be no more disappearances. At least, not from the same cause. I apologize that I am able to tell you no more than that. But let me just say, the departure of Professor Bessemer and his strange exhibition signals the end of this mystery."

Perhaps there was a sigh from the other side of the large armchair, or maybe it was just the breeze. "I shall now take any questions and enquiries you may have for our next session," the Invisible Detective declared. "Who will start us off?"

"I couldn't tell them the whole truth," Art said when everyone had gone.

Meg, Jonny and Flinch all stood at the back of the room. Jonny was counting the evening's money.

"Even if we knew the whole truth," Meg agreed.

"At least we know why she wore those braces on her legs," Art said. "She must have been one of Bessemer's first experiments."

"They all had trouble walking, didn't they?" said Jonny. "But I guess Bessemer couldn't give his new king leg irons, he had to teach it to walk properly on its own."

Art was staring into the distance. "She just wanted to be free," he said quietly. "It was my strength of will that she needed. Once Bessemer was dead and I had the lodestone, she borrowed power from my mind to try to free herself."

"She influenced you, just as Bessemer controlled her," Meg agreed gently. "He must've given her more of a mind than the others—made her almost human. She knew you would never try to control her like Bessemer did. . . ." Meg shook her head sadly. "She just wanted to get away. It wasn't your fault."

Before Art could reply, they heard the sound of footsteps coming up the stairs.

Flinch ran to look. "It's Mr. Jerrickson," she called. "Hello, Mr. Jerrickson."

The locksmith stood for a moment at the top of the stairs to catch his breath. "Missed him again, have I?" he asked. "Mr. Lake gone already?" He shook his head. "I don't know, one day I'll catch up with him, invisible or not." He smiled and nodded at the children. "What's that you've got?" he asked Art.

The others turned to look. Art was holding the stone from the display case. It caught the light from the misty window and seemed almost to glow as he turned it over in his hand. "It was in my pocket. I'd forgotten it was there. . . ."

"Do you want it?" Mr. Jerrickson asked.

Art shrugged. "I suppose not. Not really." He weighed it in his hand, then tossed it across the room.

Jerrickson caught the stone easily and examined it with an expert eye. "Might be labradorite," he said quietly. "Or not. Tell you what," he continued, looking up at Art. "If you're sure, I'll take this instead of the rent for this week. How about that?" He smiled suddenly, his face cracking into amusement. "Reckon Brandon Lake could do with a little extra money as the summer runs its course."

Flinch skipped down the stairs, keen to get back to the den. Art had promised a picnic among the rolled carpets with bread and cheese and a bottle of lemonade. Jonny was on her heels.

"Race you there," he said.

Flinch laughed. "You'll beat me easy."

"Give you a head start. I'll count to fifty."

Flinch's eyes narrowed. "A hundred," she said. "And no cheating." Before he could answer, she turned and ran.

Jonny waited at the door, shouting after her: "One, two, miss a few, ninety-nine, one hundred."

"You promised," Flinch shrieked back as Jonny dashed after her.

Art and Meg watched them go. They could hear their laughter all down the street as Jonny edged ahead of Flinch, then slowed to let her catch him up before speeding away again.

"You never told me what your dad said," Meg ventured as they started down Cannon Street after their friends.

Art considered. The evening sun was shining through Meg's hair, making it glow like fire. "It was funny," he said after a while. "He hasn't really talked about it, other than to say the prime minister sent his thanks and that Scotland Yard was following up on things."

They walked a bit further. "You said that Creepy Crabtree turned out to know nothing about it all."

Art nodded. "My dad did say one odd thing."

"Oh?"

"He said, 'I wonder what the Invisible Detective would make of this.'"

"Did you tell him?" She was pretending not to look at Art, but he could see Meg's eyes flick his way as they crossed the road. "About the Invisible Detective?"

"No." Art grinned. "Dad's seen some strange things recently, we all have. But he'd never believe that."

As they spoke, in a small room above a locksmith's shop off Cannon Street the curtains were drawn. Mr. Jerrickson, a short man with wispy gray hair that had thinned almost to nothing, stared into the depths of a strangely glowing stone through wire-rimmed pebble glasses.

And almost seventy years later, Arthur Drake blinked in surprise at his grandfather's words. But already his father was speaking again.

"I was telling him that Arthur is a good family name," he said. "This Arthur didn't even realize that we're living in your old house!"

"I remember living there with my father," Grandad said. "That house has a lot of history." His eyes were fixed on Arthur now. "I expect you're just finding that out."

"Yes," Arthur said. His throat seemed dry. He had never really wondered how old his grandfather was before. He knew his Dad was forty-eight. Grandad must be over eighty. He looked again at the crossword, at the way the capital letters in the answers were formed. Grandad's handwriting.

"I can't get three across," Grandad was saying as Arthur continued to stare at the paper. He pulled himself to his feet and walked over to join the boy, looking down at the clues. "I did think it might be 'puppet show,' but that's too many letters."

Arthur looked up sharply. Something his father had just said was echoing in his mind as he looked into Grandad's eyes. "What did Dad mean—'this Arthur'?" he asked.

"I thought you knew," Dad replied from across the room. "I told you Arthur is an old family name." He laughed. "Arthur Drake, meet your namesake."

Grandad's mouth twitched with amusement and the wrinkles around his eyes seemed to deepen. Arthur just stared. "You mean . . ."

"It doesn't say 'Grandad' on his birth certificate, does it!" Dad smiled. "You were named after him."

"Arthur Drake," Arthur said, so quietly he could barely hear his own voice.

"That's right," Grandad replied in a voice that was almost as quiet. "But my friends call me Art for short."